THE WRITER'S
TABLE

Aidan

your story is waiting to be told my friend
find your writing table and begin

THE WRITER'S
TABLE

JULIAN SIMMONS

ISBN-13: 9780692378229

ISBN-10: 0692378227

Cover design by Megan Katsanevakis

For my wife, Jen, and our children, Julian, Juno, and Jude. I hope our writing table takes us on many more adventures.

For my mother, Shirley, and the sacrifices you made so I could dream.

And to Robert Hopkins for the creative freedom you gave me as a child that I have always kept close to my heart.

CONTENTS

PROLOGUE

My parents were avid readers, and from the time I was born, they made it a ritual to read a story to me before bed. Over the years, we progressed from tales by the Brothers Grimm and Hans Christian Andersen to novels by Melville and Dickens. I loved reading, and since we moved from the busy city life of the West Coast to the relaxed beaches of the East, I had a lot of time to lounge and read books.

About the time I was eight years old, I spent many afternoons at a place called Fiddler's Point reading anything my school library would loan me. Fiddler's Point was a narrow piece of land that stretched into the marsh near our house, a peninsula that jetted out past our waterfront home and beyond the oyster grass and cattails that nearby fiddler crabs used as a playground. *My* playground was at the tip of the land, far enough from the house so that no one would notice me, and that suited me just fine. I liked the isolation.

I was an only child who lived with my parents on a secluded piece of property we shared with my grandpa. Our houses were separated by a small, dense set of trees. Although there were plenty of places to be alone, it was Fiddler's Point that I liked the most.

After each Christmas, my father would drag the Christmas tree down to Fiddler's Point with every intention of lighting it on fire, but

I always stopped him and used it as a makeshift sofa or bed. I mashed the branches down and covered them with palm fronds that had fallen off some of the nearby palmetto trees. This was a place where my mind was relaxed, where I could take a book and envelop myself in whatever place I read about.

Fiddler's Point reminded me of a deserted island. No one ever bothered me, and aside from the annual Christmas tree dumping by my father and the occasional visits from Grandpa, no one else ever came out there.

Grandpa was the one who first brought me to Fiddler's Point. We walked along the path leading to the end of the peninsula looking for bullet shells. He told me there was once a great battle there. A giant squid king tried to take the surrounding land from the fishermen who left the docks every day in search of the squid's magical ink, and one fisherman almost got his hands on it.

Legend said the ink had power beyond any man, a potion that could create worlds men only dream of. A single drop would bring the entire world's fortunes to one's feet, and it was for that very reason the squid king protected his magical ink. He saw men as creatures that destroyed everything they touched, and he feared possession of the ink would bring about an unstable world.

The squid king created a powerful storm, a hurricane, to drown the fishermen. In an epic battle, the squid king and the hurricane besieged Fiddler's Point. The fishermen tried to kill the squid king with guns, bombs, and harpoons, but they couldn't defeat him. In the many years since the battle, all that was left were old shotgun shells and rotting wooden boats that sat in the marsh.

The story of the squid king stuck with me and made me fall in love with Fiddler's Point. There was something about it that made me feel like I was part of the epic battle just by being there. Even though the story was only make-believe, I wondered what side of the battlefield I would have been on. I wondered if I would have protected what was rightfully the squid king's or if I would have been too curious about what fortunes the ink could bring me, so much that I would fight to the death for it.

One summer night, I learned of a new part to the story of the squid king and its connection to *The Lonely Tree*, a story that Grandpa often read to me when I was little. To me, the two stories seemed unlikely to ever be part of the same larger tale, but Grandpa easily convinced me that there was no reason they couldn't.

I sat in my bed next to my father, eagerly waiting for him to begin reading. The window was open, a breeze blew through the screen, and it felt cool against my warm cheeks. The air smelled of a fresh rain that had passed over our house, and tree frogs were chirping in the nearby oak trees. I pulled the covers over my lap and pushed the book toward him.

"Not this book again. Aren't you a little too old for this one?" he asked.

"Yes, but I want you to read it anyway. I like the voices you make."

My father enchanted every story by performing different dialects for the characters. I was intrigued by the way certain letters rolled off his tongue as he transformed from a Spanish-speaking horsefly named Santiago to a French butterfly named Pierre.

My father was tall and slim with short, curly brown hair. Large, black, rectangular glasses rested on his pointy nose. He was a freelance artist and occasionally sold some of his work to friends of Grandpa, but he earned a regular paycheck by teaching graphic design at a community college. He spent most of his time painting or wandering through the woods next to our house, "being one with nature," as he often said. It was in the woods where he practiced different voices for the characters in my books.

"Tha leetle tree said to dee butterfly, 'Whut ez most emportant to yu?'" my father asked as Pierre.

I smiled at him and looked back to the book. A single tree swayed back and forth and smiled upon the butterfly, which talked to a passing horsefly. An orange and gold sky against a green meadow illuminated the page. I closed my eyes. The colors burned into my memory as I listened to my father continue reading.

He was near the end of the book—my favorite part—when I opened my eyes and looked at the page. Near the lakeshore stood the budding tulip tree that couldn't have been higher than my head. The moon reflected off dewy blades of grass.

I closed my eyes again and tried to imagine myself there, letting the scene take form around me. The petals on the tree began to flutter. The water rippled and shimmered under the glowing moon. I heard loons close by and waves lapping along the edge of the shore.

It felt real.

I reached my hand out to touch the tree, but the image undulated like a hologram. Everything was moving and alive, yet I couldn't go anywhere or touch anything. I closed my eyes and focused on the sound of the lake.

"What's going on in here?" a voice called from down the hall, bringing me back to reality.

My grandpa had stopped by to say hello. Grandpa Rowe was my dad's father. His name was Colvin, he taught English at the university, and when he wasn't grading papers, he was fishing or writing in one of his many journals.

"Did you catch any fish today?" I asked.

"A few snapper, and you wouldn't believe this, but one of them had a tiny squid in its mouth."

"A squid?" said my father.

"Slimy little thing. What are you guys reading?" Grandpa said. He looked at the back of the book my father was holding. "Ah, *The Lonely Tree*, I see. Your dad do the voices?"

I nodded.

"It's funny how you're reading that story *and* I caught a squid today."

"How is that funny?" I asked.

My father got out of the bed and made room for Grandpa.

"I'm just going to go close the garage doors. I'll leave you two to it," my father said, then he left the room.

"Didn't I tell you the story about the squid king?"

"Yes, of course, but what does that have to do with *The Lonely Tree?*" I asked.

Grandpa propped himself up against the headboard, removed his reading glasses, and cleaned them with his shirt.

"Well, the lonely tree was the squid king's creation. It was all that was left after the Battle of Fiddler's Point."

"What? You never told me that part of the story."

"Well, shall I tell you?"

I nodded and positioned my back against the adjacent wall so I could watch him head-on.

"After the Battle of Fiddler's Point was over, there was nothing left of the seaside community. Everything had been destroyed. Houses sat deserted, their broken windows resembling someone with missing teeth. Trees were snapped in half, and the sides of buildings were painted in pluff mud, marking how high the water rose. The squid king sat in the creek examining his destruction. He was about to turn and leave when he saw a boy stumble down the road. The boy was eight years old, the same age you are now. When his eyes locked with the squid king's, the boy began to run toward him, begging him to wait. The boy's hands reached toward the squid king while he ran down the path.

"'There's nothing left of my town. I have no home. There's no one left to help me. Please, undo what you have done!' the boy cried.

"The king looked at the boy in anger and shook his head. 'Your townsmen brought this on themselves. They should have never tried to take what wasn't theirs,' he told the boy.

"The boy fell to his knees into a puddle of murky water, exhausted from the storm.

"The boy pleaded again and then passed out from exhaustion. The squid king was not easily persuaded, but the sight of a young child begging for a resolution softened his anger. The squid king reflected on his wrath, and he began to feel foolish for his actions. From thin air he pulled a tiny medicine vial and bottled a few drops of ink from his eyes.

"He scooped the child up in his tentacles and poured the ink into the boy's mouth. The boy immediately awoke but lay motionless in the

6

arms of the king. With another tentacle, the squid king bottled a few more ink drops and wrapped the boy's hands around it.

"'Take this bottle and with it you will be able to rebuild your town,' the squid king whispered in the boy's ear. He placed the boy back on the ground, and without another word between the two, he retreated back into the sea.

"The boy walked back to where his home once stood. Among broken bits of his house, he heard a voice within that told him to pour the ink from the bottle onto the ground. Within seconds, a small tree grew, and the boy felt a strong connection to it, as if the tree had grown from his own body. The boy watched as purple tulips sprouted from the branches, and with each tulip, the boy felt stronger.

"Inspired by his encounter with the squid king and the creation of the tree, he began to write several stories. Season after season, the tree stayed the same, never losing its leaves or flowers and never growing taller than the boy was when it first grew. Over the years, the boy shared his stories with anyone who would listen, and with the fame of the never-changing shrub, the town slowly began to rebuild itself around the tree.

"Decades went by, and small cottages were torn down for planned housing developments that made way for city landscapes and high-rise apartment buildings. The boy grew older too, but he never forgot about the tree. He rallied every now and then to have it preserved, until one day he disappeared. Some thought he moved away or died, but no one could ever confirm their suspicions.

"The tree remained, but its fame faded and the city crumbled. Jobs disappeared, and the livelihood of the town diminished, allowing nature to take back what once was. Streets vanished beneath rolling hills of grass, and tall lush trees stretched their branches toward the sky. No one noticed that the once booming town had all but vanished within just a few years of the man's disappearance. Time kept moving, and the lonely tree looked just like any ordinary sapling in a field in the countryside."

Grandpa paused and cleared his throat.

"Then what happened?" I asked.

"That's it. Hence *The Lonely Tree*. We now pick up where my story leaves off," Grandpa said. "Hey, I'm going to try to get some early morning fishing in. You want to go with me?"

Fishing with anyone but my grandpa was boring. With him, I could expect to hear many fascinating stories. After connecting the story of the squid king and *The Lonely Tree*, his invitation was a perfect opportunity to find out more about the magical tree.

"Sure. I'll go with you."

He threw the bed sheet over my head.

"I'll pick you up at seven thirty."

I smiled at him.

"Hey, real quick. Where were you born? How old are you? And what's your favorite childhood memory?" Grandpa asked.

Grandpa always asked me the same three questions every time we saw each other.

"I was born in Dunes City, Oregon, I'm eight years old, and my favorite childhood memory is our trip to the Redwood Forest."

He laughed and gave me a thumbs-up before leaving my room.

PROLOGUE

I once asked my mom why Grandpa always asked me those questions, and she said he posed the same questions to her as well.

"It's probably because he is getting old and more forgetful," she would respond.

But Grandpa was not the forgetful kind. His mind was quite sharp. During one fishing trip just last month, we came across a fish I had never seen before and neither had anyone else on the boat, but Grandpa knew exactly what kind it was.

"That there is a rare Atlantic short-nosed sturgeon. They live in saltwater but spawn in freshwater rivers," Grandpa said as if reciting from a textbook on aquatic life.

He never forgot my birthday or my parents' wedding anniversary, he was never stumped by any of the complicated math problems I brought home from school, and he never faltered at reciting lines of poetry by Whitman, Angelou, or Poe.

What I found most profound about his memory was his ability to understand the means of time. The man was never late for anything and knew exactly when to leave his house to arrive at any destination on time. If the boat left at 10:00 a.m., he knew we would have to leave the house by 9:50 a.m. to allow enough time to walk to the boat ramp and load our things.

Not only that, but everything he did prior to 9:50 a.m. was also calculated. He would begin brushing his teeth five minutes before we left, he began packing our lunch ten minutes before that, and so on until the precision of timed events led up to our departure. There was nothing wrong with his memory, and although it felt like I had every intention of finding out why he asked me the same three questions, I always seemed to forget about it moments later.

✶ ✶ ✶

The next day, I woke up early and prepared myself for a morning of fishing. I packed a bag with a few snacks from the cupboard along with sunscreen and a book just in case Grandpa didn't feel up to telling stories.

I waited for him on the front steps and checked my watch every few minutes.

7:29 a.m.

Grandpa was usually punctual, so I stood up and looked down the driveway, expecting him to arrive any second.

7:30 a.m.

I walked to the road that connected our houses, but it was quiet. Only the squirrels were moving about, foraging in the trees.

7:33 a.m.

There was still no sign of him, so I walked back up to the house and sat down on the front steps. I pulled out my book. After reading just a few pages, I checked my watch again.

7:43 a.m.

It was unlike my grandpa to be late. I questioned if I'd heard him correctly the night before but assured myself he did indeed say 7:30 a.m.

I walked back inside and called his house, but he didn't answer. I placed the phone back on the receiver and decided I would just walk to his house. I took the path through the woods that connected our properties.

8:00 a.m.

When I arrived at Grandpa's house, I found his garage door open and his car parked just outside it. The trailer holding the boat sat unattached next to the distant shed. As I made my way through the garage, I passed all of Grandpa's fishing poles still in their holders. I entered the house and called to him.

"Grandpa?"

There was no sound, so I started to make my way through the house.

"Grandpa, it's Alden. Are you home?"

There was no response. Only silence. Nothing looked out of place or suspicious. His mail was neatly stacked on the counter. The stools at the bar where he normally drank his morning coffee were tucked underneath the counter in a straight line. His bed was made, and the only light on in the house was the one on his desk. Everything seemed as it should, except Grandpa was nowhere to be found.

I thought he must have gone for a walk, so I grabbed a pen and decided to leave him a note.

When I got home, I placed my bag by the front door and camped out in front of the TV, feeling positive Grandpa would be along shortly to take me fishing.

Around 10:00 a.m., my parents got out of bed.

"Oh, Alden, I didn't know you were still here. I thought you were going fishing with Grandpa," my mother said.

"So did I, but he never showed up. I even walked to his house, but he wasn't there. I left him a note."

Hours went by, and there was still no sign of Grandpa.

"Still no word?" my father asked.

"No," I said. "Don't you think that's a little weird?"

My father agreed and picked up the phone to call Grandpa's house, but no one picked up on the other end.

"No answer?" I said.

He shook his head. "I'm going to walk over there."

"Okay, I'll come with you."

When we arrived, everything looked the same as it had when I walked over earlier. We searched the house, but still, Grandpa was nowhere to be found.

"I'm sure he just went out for a walk and forgot about the time. You know how he loves to explore the property," my father said.

Back at our house, my father paced the front walkway.

"I'm just going to walk around the property and see if I can find him. Tell your mother."

Inside, my mother was on the phone. I decided to wait for her in my room. I jumped into the ball of sheets clumped on my bed. My head hit the book my father read to me the previous night, *The Lonely Tree*. I took it in my hands, leaned back on my pillow, and stared at the front cover. Its laminated coating reflected the midday sun. I thought about what happened the night before, when I suddenly felt like I was in the book as my father was reading it.

I opened the book, turned a few pages, and stopped at an image of a doe and her fawn. They were drinking from a lake in a field surrounded by trees and overgrown bushes bursting with red berries. I slowly closed my eyes. Just like the night before, the image was fading when suddenly I could see the deer's ears twitch and the lake's small waves break on the shore where the deer were drinking.

I reached toward the ground and tried to touch the grass. I needed validation that this was real. When I reached out, my fingers never met the tips of the grass, and instead they extended into nothing. The scene in front of me rippled, proving once again this was all just an illusion. Feeling frustrated, I let out a defeated sigh. As I exhaled, the doe looked right at me.

The sound of something cracking in the surrounding brush startled both deer, and they darted away and into the forest.

THE ASSIGNMENT

Two years passed without a trace of Grandpa. My ninth and tenth birthdays had come and gone without him. He usually helped me plan the most extravagant birthday parties and would proclaim, "You only turn seven once!" or "You only turn eight once!" I missed him, and with each passing day, I felt doubtful I'd ever hear his voice again.

There were no leads, no trace of a kidnapping, nothing. It was as if he'd vanished into thin air. The stress of not knowing what happened to him took my father's attention from our bedtime ritual, and instead of reading books together, we searched online police reports.

My father stopped painting and spent most of his days searching the surrounding woods. I knew he desperately wanted to find Grandpa, but it was useless. At dusk each day he came into the house looking defeated.

"Anything?" I'd ask.

He'd just shrug and say, "No."

THE ASSIGNMENT

The more he searched the depths of the woods, the more depressed he became. Each day his response got weaker, and eventually his vocal responses gave way to barely a shrug.

My mother tried to be supportive by going with him on his searches, but then she too came back feeling bemused and helpless. The sadness was heavy, recognizable by the slow grumbles we made when passing one another on our way to our own rooms of isolation. The happiness slowly faded from our family. I watched a lot of TV. I stopped hanging out with my friends and became a recluse. Being a loner meant I got bullied, and within a few months, I was making routine visits to the principal's office.

The fights were always my fault, according to the principal. Every other week I sat across from a new bully while the principal noted I was the only common theme to each visit. I started to believe her, and after the fifth meeting in her office, I started making up excuses to stay home so I could avoid everyone at school. Soon, though, my parents caught on and sent me back to school, where I found out the bullies had moved on to new kids to pick on. A part of me became a little jealous that I was no longer of any interest to them. I slowly became invisible.

I stayed up late and listened to depressing music. Anything with a violin or a song played in a minor key immediately evoked tears. I daydreamed of a different life—a life of happiness, a life of color and magic. I fantasized about having the ability to fly, manipulate wind, or make people love me. I ruled vast kingdoms from castles, traveled the world, and helped anyone I crossed who was in need. All of it was just thoughts in my head. In real life, my voice was changing, I was growing taller, and my face was breaking out. My parents cast their attention to these changes and called them out when running into people at the grocery store.

"Yep, he's going through the change," my mother would say to the cashier.

"Our little boy is not so little anymore. Right, son?" my father would say to the pharmacist.

Grandpa's disappearance amplified my anxiety. While I was eating breakfast or riding the bus, I wondered where Grandpa was. I imagined him living with a different family in another country, or worse, his body rotting in a secluded forest. I tried to push the darker scenarios from my mind and imagined coming home one day to see him pop up from behind the counter and shout, "Surprise! I'm back!"

My grades slipped, and distractions became more prominent. Brushing my teeth, eating, doing homework, watching TV, and even sleeping became difficult. My mind was uncontrollably filled with whimsical ideas, as if it were on cruise control. Even stranger was the way my mind would create places. I would be watching a soccer game on TV and suddenly the players were kicking a giant tangerine down a field on the surface of the ocean.

My parents were so concerned by my grades and general disconnection to life that they sent me to a psychiatrist. I spent my Friday nights in an office, being questioned by a man who constantly morphed into a large teddy bear. Medication was prescribed to me, which only made me feel like some kind of lab experiment.

It wasn't just me checking out, though. The whole family was on constant edge and hoped that at any moment someone would call and tell us they found Grandpa. But hope was squashed when Grandpa's house was sold and all his belongings were moved into our garage. It felt a little like closure, but without really knowing what happened, the door was always going to be open.

Grandpa's disappearance seemed to have taken the biggest toll on my father. "He always seemed to be battling a cough or cold, and he had to make frequent visits to the doctor." He would have one or two weeks of good health but would then somehow relapse. The time in between his illnesses became progressively shorter as one ailment connected with the next.

I was in my last year of elementary school when things started to change again.

My fifth-grade teacher, Mr. Brevard, gave my class an unorthodox assignment. This was Mr. Brevard's fourth year at Greyside Elementary School. He was young, in his mid-twenties. He was quite different from the majority of the faculty, who sported denim ankle-length skirts and seemed to have obtained their teaching degrees when Lincoln was president. He was known among students as the "cool" teacher, and getting into his class was like winning the lottery. I didn't have to play the lottery that year to get into his class, though. Mr. Brevard had been good friends with Grandpa.

He had been one of Grandpa's students in college, and they had kept in close contact with each other over the years. Grandpa often brought Mr. Brevard along on our fishing trips, and when Grandpa first disappeared, he came to visit just about every day. Over the years since Grandpa's disappearance, Mr. Brevard's visits became less frequent. I thought by being in his class that we would swap stories of past fishing excursions with Grandpa, relive all the good times we had with him, but it was the complete opposite. It was as if we were strangers. He never initiated any such conversation about our common link outside of school, and I was too shy. Our relationship had become strictly between teacher and student.

One day Mr. Brevard handed out black-and-white composition books. A collective groan stirred the room. How many lines of text would I have to fill before turning in something that would be even less enjoyable for him to read than it would be for me to write?

Mr. Brevard informed us that this would be an ongoing project. The class groaned again. Every week we were to write in our notebooks. We could write about whatever we wanted: the weather, our favorite pet, a current event. Whatever came to our minds, we would put it in our composition books.

I'd never had a teacher give an assignment that required only putting pen to paper. It was liberating for someone my age to be given such freedom. Up to this point in school, I had accepted that no teacher would ever ask for anything other than what was written in our textbooks.

To get started, Mr. Brevard said he would play a song on the stereo and we would write what the song made us think about, how it made us feel. We could write whatever filled our minds.

I pulled out a pen and watched as he placed the CD into the player and hit play. The class went silent, and smiles spread across our faces in response to our teacher's eccentric approach to writing. I felt exhilarated, and I held my pen ready as the song started to play, but as the first few notes rang through the classroom, I stopped and became distracted by watching the other students.

THE ASSIGNMENT

Mia Benson was one of six students who shared the large, six-foot-long table with me. She sat directly across from me and was writing feverishly. She was by far the most artistic person in my class. Her most recent sculpture of the city's bridge, made entirely out of seashells, won the tenth-annual Young Artist Award given by the city. She was never happy unless she finished assignments before everyone else, and this new challenge was not going to be any different. She called it her "wow factor." She believed teachers always remembered the first and last things they graded and everything else in between was just filler. And it worked. Teachers used her work as examples for what everyone else should strive for. The song was about a minute in, and Mia had already filled half a page.

One of our table partners, Tommy Fits, had done the opposite. He was writing in big letters and had filled his paper with two sentences. He had already closed the composition book and tossed his pen on top.

Angela Spade sat next to me and wrote in neat cursive so small I was sure Mr. Brevard would ask her to just tell him what she wrote.

I didn't immediately start writing. I found it strange how easily my mind could drift off to faraway places when I was supposed to be in the moment—yet there I was being asked to deliberately drift off and I was unable to think of anything other than what my classmates were doing.

I listened to the music, which sounded slow and sad. I wrote a couple of paragraphs in my composition book and then closed my eyes. I envisioned the words I wrote about, and suddenly I found myself standing in complete darkness. As the music picked up the pace, a light ahead grew bigger and enveloped me.

The light dimmed, and I saw my doppelganger standing at the edge of a grassy cliff. A single palm tree stood near the edge, and my clone sat beneath it, dangling one foot over the edge. I watched the sunset bring an orange and pink sky toward me. I felt what my doppelganger was feeling.

A slight breeze wisped through his hair and rustled the palm fronds, breaking the silence. I felt the cool, soft texture of the grass beneath his legs against my own skin. He closed his eyes and leaned back into the rough tree trunk.

A piano crescendo came and then faded as the sun disappeared below the ocean. As soon as the sun faded, a loud cackle echoed beneath the cliff. My other self leaned over, and I saw what he saw. A skeleton face looked up at me and grinned. He then let out another chilling cackle that startled me.

I opened my eyes and saw the entire class looking at me.

"Are you okay?" Angela asked.

"Yes, why?"

"I think you fell asleep, and you just jumped out of your chair."

"I did?"

She nodded.

"Everything okay over there?" asked Mr. Brevard.

"He's fine," Angela responded.

It was odd that my vision felt real—as real as when my father read *The Lonely Tree* to me the night before Grandpa disappeared. In the crazy aftermath of Grandpa's disappearance, I had forgotten about how real that vision was to me. This vision felt the same, though. Everything around me was moving and alive, but I couldn't move.

THE ASSIGNMENT

A new song began, and I tried to forget about what I had just seen. I wrote a few more paragraphs, but this time I changed the scene. I closed my eyes again and envisioned the words I wrote. Just as before, I found myself in complete darkness and then a light grew bigger and enveloped me.

I stood alone at a bus stop. Down the street I saw an approaching bus that slammed on the brakes at every stop sign. As the bus approached, it slowed to a crawl before stopping so the bus door was directly in front of me. I looked through the door and did not see anyone driving the bus.

I wanted to investigate further, but found I could not move. Unexpectedly, the bus slowly started to move forward again, and I eagerly peered into each window, looking for any sign of a passenger. Window after window was empty, only displaying the reflection of the houses behind me. As the last window approached, I saw the same skeleton face emerge from the depths of the dark bus, and once its face was fully visible, it let out another cackle.

I jolted awake and found the entire class staring at me again.

"Will you stop falling asleep?" Angela said as she pulled my shirt.

"I'm sorry."

"Everything still okay over there? Alden, are you feeling all right?" Mr. Brevard asked.

"I'm fine, thanks."

Everyone went back to writing, except Angela, who stared at me with concern.

"What's wrong?" she asked.

"I just saw the strangest thing."

I searched the words on my paper, and everything in the story I'd written was as I saw it in my vision, except the creepy skeleton face. I couldn't figure out where it had come from.

"Don't close your eyes. You need to finish this assignment before you get in trouble," said Angela.

I brushed off the skeleton from my mind and tried to focus on the assignment.

The music continued to play in the background, and I tried to clear my head, but the skeleton face was now overpowering thoughts of anything else. Still, I gave it one more shot. This time I opened my eyes and I was standing at Fiddler's Point. Broken reeds lay near the pile of old Christmas trees, and the tide was far out in the ocean. I scanned the wetlands, and my eyes stopped when I saw the skeleton standing as still as a rock in the middle of the marsh, staring back at me. The same cackle raced toward me, and I jolted awake.

"Okay, that's it," Angela said as she put her pen down. "Clearly something is wrong with you. You look as pale as a ghost."

"You sure you're okay, Alden?" Mr. Brevard asked.

"I'm fine."

The bell rang, and everyone gathered their belongings. The music had stopped, and in its place the rustling of papers being shoved into book bags filled the air.

Week after week I tried to write, but I couldn't because of the fear of seeing the skeleton figure again. My classmates shared their stories with one another, but I always lied and said my story wasn't finished yet. Sometimes Mr. Brevard would call on someone to read what he or she wrote, and this terrified me. I didn't want to lie to my teacher, but I always prepared an excuse in my head just in case he did call on me:

I left it in my desk yesterday.

It's in my mother's car.

My father has it because I asked him to proof it first.

I often wondered if I should have just written a collection of excuses not to write, so then at least I would have something written. Mr. Brevard never told us when he was going to collect our notebooks, and since he let me off the hook once, I was sure to get in trouble if I didn't have a single thing written by the time he made a second collection.

But it never failed. I sat on my bed with my composition book open every Sunday night, a million thoughts in my head, but not one of them ever managed to leap onto one of the blank pages, too scared to leave the safety of my mind.

We were approaching our Thanksgiving break when Mr. Brevard asked me to stay after class.

"Alden, I noticed you haven't been turning in any writing assignments."

"I don't know what to write," I lied.

"You can write about anything!"

I shrugged.

"So how come you haven't turned anything in?"

"I don't know," I said, and looked away.

He then handed me a blue cloth spiral-bound notebook. It was nothing like the boring black-and-white composition books sold to the masses at the beginning of every school year. Inside the book were pages of thick, cream-colored paper packed with scribbled text and black ink sketches of trees and grassy fields.

I hovered over the drawings of tall oaks and weeping willows. There were pages and pages of trees in the summer, packed with leafy stems, and there were trees by snowy riverbanks, leafless and stiff as rocks. As my eyes traced the horizon of an empty meadow, I thought of the skeleton figure standing in the marsh. I closed the book.

"No, I can't," I said.

"You can't what?"

"I just can't write anything. My head is too clouded."

Mr. Brevard pulled his chair to the other side of the desk and sat down to face me.

"I had a problem writing as a kid, too. My parents were going through a divorce, and the only thing I could think of writing about was how sad I was and all the fighting between my mom and dad."

"This isn't like that," I interrupted.

Mr. Brevard continued, "So I started writing about all my feelings anyway, and after reading it, the pain was too real. The pain I wrote about was as alive as you or me…"

My attention sparked at his words. I thought he was describing exactly how my words came alive whenever I re-envisioned them.

"Then I tried adding a counter-element to my entries. My pain was alive for a little while, but then it was vanquished by something new and powerful. Something so extraordinary it made all the pain and grief disappear. For me, that element was trees. You can see from my journal there are trees on almost every page. They're there to capture any pain I wrote about, sucked up and solidified in each branch and leaf. My fears were no longer a threat thanks to my trees. Notice, however, the trees still exist, meaning your pain and fears never completely go away, but they can be stopped and contained by whatever element you choose to use."

From under the table he brought out a bright red cloth notebook like his blue one and slid it in front of me.

"This is for you," he said.

"So I don't have to use this old composition book?"

"No, of course not. I gave those to everyone because it was the cheapest and easiest way to get everyone to do the assignment."

"And I can include drawings too?"

"Drawings, photographs, of course! Whatever you want," Mr. Brevard said excitedly. "I took the liberty of drawing you one of my trees. You can use it as a counter-element until you think of one of your own."

I left his class wondering if it would work. I wondered if I could write again and be protected from the skeleton figure by using the tree Mr. Brevard drew.

THE WRITER'S TABLE

When I got home, I looked around and hoped the perfect writing spot would jump out at me. I went into the kitchen and sat at the table, but the faucet dripped, distracting me. I went into my room, but the cat was on my desk. I sat on the front steps, but my back hurt. I drifted to the garage. It was a two-story detachment with an upstairs loft full of windows. My father spent a lot of time there reading and painting. Grandpa's furniture now filled what space was left, but I was sure there had to be somewhere for me to write up there.

I opened the door and climbed the wooden stairs to the second floor, where a warm, musty mothball-and-caramel smell hit me. I slid some of the furniture out of the way and made a path to the other side of the room. I propped open a few windows to allow the cool autumn breeze to aerate the loft, and the fresh scent of pine from the trees behind the garage filtered into the room. Three long shelves lined a back wall and were cluttered with paint jars, blank canvases, and brushes.

THE WRITER'S TABLE

This was the place I needed to be. The paint spatters on the shelves and walls gave the impression that creativity had literally exploded there. The large windows made the loft seem twice its size. A soft red beanbag chair looked comfortable, so I sat down with my book and started writing, but after a few seconds the sound of the beans shifting inside the bag distracted me. I stretched and looked around the room for another spot. There was a lot of furniture covered by thick blue quilts, and I wondered what was hiding under them. What pieces of Grandpa's life were being preserved under all of these blankets?

I peeked under a few and saw several familiar items that used to be in Grandpa's house. There were a couple of tufted chairs, a bench, a few small dressers, and a wooden desk that was by far the largest piece of furniture, as it towered over the other pieces. I took a second glance at the desk and noticed its large, bowed hutch, and with the blue blanket on top, it resembled a massive tidal wave approaching the shoreline, ready to take out anything in its path. All the furniture had been pushed together in the center, and the desk was on the outer edge, making it easy to get to. The top of the desk had several cracks, and deep within the ridges something shiny caught the sunlight coming in from the windows. It looked like some kind of liquid had spilled in between the crevices and hardened. The desk was old, like Grandpa had been before he disappeared, and I imagined him sitting at it writing letters to friends, grading papers, and paying bills like my parents did at our dining table.

I pulled the desk away from the other furniture and positioned it beside the window. Another breeze came through, and I pulled a chair up to the desk. I slid my hand across it, and the cracks caught the creases in my palm.

A splinter stuck in my skin, reminding me of my first encounter with the desk. I had played underneath it and pretended it was my house when I was younger. Grandpa chased me out, and I accidentally cut my hand on the side. He asked me what had happened, and through my tears I told him his desk had hurt me. He wiped my tears away and said it was no ordinary desk. It was his writing table, and it was just trying to reach out to say hello.

The writing table was unique, unlike anything I had ever seen. The top of the desk was shallow, and there were several breaks in the wood. You couldn't put a single piece of paper on top and begin writing. The paper would easily tear against the wood when pressed by a pen or pencil. The hutch contained several tiny drawers, none of which would open when I tried. The hutch bowed in the middle, making the center drawers large and square and the outer drawers small and uneven.

The legs were large, and the feet swirled at the bottom like the cones of snail shells. The front two legs looked like they were made of the horns of a rhinoceros, black and hard as cement.

Two drawers flanked the middle of the table in the shape of the letter *P* resting horizontally. The most striking feature rested in the center of the two middle drawers. A round, glass-encased clock ticked quietly. The face yellowed beneath bronzed numbers.

With the windows open and the air in the loft cleared, I could smell the natural wood of the tabletop. The aroma was distinctly that of oak, which is why the table must have felt so heavy. I placed my notebook on the tabletop and opened to a fresh page and began to write:

It was a sunny afternoon, and in the quiet of an open field, green blades of grass leaned forward and backward as the wind brushed the hillside. In the distance a single oak tree stood on top of a steep hill with an old wooden swing attached. The oak tree stood out among the apple orchard where fruit hung in the sunlight.

I kept the writing simple and reality-based. I didn't want to create an unfamiliar world with mythical creatures or talking animals that might fuel the possibility of the skeleton figure returning. After a few minutes, I had written a couple of paragraphs and decided to proof-read them.

Then, just as I had done before in class, I closed my eyes and envisioned the place I'd just written about, only this time the room shook. I opened my eyes, and all around me shimmering pieces of light exploded like someone lit a thousand sparklers. I held onto the writing table in fear of falling through the floor. Shards of light swirled around me, but they didn't seem to be touching me or the table.

Within a few seconds, the light subsided and I found myself alone, sitting at the writing table in a field, the vast field with apple trees from my story. In the distance I saw the oak tree with the wooden swing—the same tree and swing I had described. The field was more beautiful than I imagined when I was writing about it. The grass was green and plush. The apples were so bright I could see them from hundreds of feet away. They sparkled in the sunlight.

I was still unsure how I came to this place. The only things that came with me were the writing table and the chair I sat in. The note-book I'd been writing in was nowhere to be found. I pushed my chair back and noticed the hands of the clock on the writing table were spinning furiously. In the center of the hands where a bronze pin previously held them together, there was something silver. I leaned down and saw it was some kind of electricity, something sparking, very similar to the shards of light that brought me to the field.

This experience felt different from my previous visits to one of my stories. Here I was able to move around, and the dirt and grass were real, not an illusion like before. I walked around the writing table and knelt down to run the grass through my fingers. I wondered if my new ability to move around made me more vulnerable to objects moving toward me, objects like the skeleton figure. I searched for any sign of him and patiently waited to see if he appeared. A few minutes went by, and all was still clear. Perhaps Mr. Brevard's tree suggestion prevented the skeleton from entering my story, but I was still unsure. Although I knew this story to be the one I wrote about, to experience it first-hand made me feel as if it was my first time in a foreign land. I cautiously made my way to the center of the field.

There was nothing around me except the wind blowing through the nearby trees. Every few minutes I searched the grounds for the skeleton, but he never appeared. The air got warmer and my body became less tense. The solitude was inviting and reminded me of Fiddler's Point. I imagined myself lying in the grass reading a book, the sun warming my face and then being cooled by sporadic graces of wind. It was just me and nature. A sense of safety and happiness came over me. This was a place created in my imagination, and now it was in front of me. It was real.

Away from the writing table, I ran across the field and stopped at the oak tree and grabbed the twisted rope of the swing. I positioned myself on the seat and kicked off the ground. My gaze followed the rope as it wound up the tree branch, intertwining itself among the thick stems.

THE WRITER'S TABLE

The leaves fluttered in the warm breeze, as if waving to a friend to come over.

As I swung through the air, I noticed that behind me there was nothing but white space. It was as if the world I created stopped just beyond the oak tree. It went on forever, no end in sight. I did not remember describing anything beyond the oak tree, so I assumed it was empty for that very reason. If I was able to create a place like this, I imagined it would not be hard to create something truly bewildering.

I walked back to the table and thought about the logistics of how I got to my story—and, more complicated, how to get back. I examined the table. Nothing stood out as a method for taking me home. I retraced my steps: I was sitting at the writing table, my notebook was in front of me, and I was imagining what I had written. I had everything except my notebook. I was in the middle of visualizing what I'd written when I was transported to the field, so I imagined myself sitting back in the loft. Then shards of light engulfed me and I was back among Grandpa's furniture. Upon my return, I was surprised to see my notebook sitting on top of the writing table as if it had been there all along.

Excited by my newfound ability, I wanted proof that what I wrote about was a place I could physically visit again, so I decided to write a little more to test my theory. I stuck to continuing the same story, but decided this time to add a bit of pure fantasy.

Beyond the oak tree a small pond was nestled in the middle of a quaint valley. A bright yellow canoe hovered above the glassy water, examining its reflection. The branches of the nearby weeping willow parted to reveal a beautiful white swan whose feathers sparkled as if a hundred twinkling stars had been cast upon her.

31

I put the pen down and read the words in my notebook. Again, the room began to shake and exploded into pieces of light. And just as before, I landed in the story I had written. This time the writing table landed on the other side of the field. Since this was a continuation of the story, I was now able to see both the field and the pond.

Everything was just as I'd written it: the sparkling swan walked through the willow, and the yellow canoe hovered above the pond.

I felt powerful. I could create anything I wanted.

I spent the next few days going back and forth, writing and traveling to the places I wrote about, places that came to life only when I sat at the writing table. My imagination ran wild: I created variations of the field with the apple trees and swing. I walked through fields made of marshmallows. I sprouted wings and soared high above trees that blew in the wind like the florets of a dandelion. Flop-eared baby rabbits foraged for carrots made of gold. Bright purple bird eggs made roads of solid rock when thrown on the ground. I created the utopia of my youth: animals, objects, and places that were beautiful, magical, warm, and safe.

My field led to moonlit beaches and underwater parks where seahorses playfully charged a fever of stingrays. Forests made of giant broccoli opened to moving hills of colossal strawberries.

My everyday life and my fantasy world began to blur. Some days I didn't think I would ever return. My parents wondered where I was off to, and each time my made-up answers got trickier. During the school week I bolted home after class and ventured off with the writing table.

I made up my own ideal classroom in my stories, which was often outdoors, under large canopies of maple leaves the size of airplanes. My classmates were a troop of kangaroos, our teacher a large brown owl with specks of white dots whom I called Mr. Hoots. I loved animals and used them a lot in my writing. It wasn't until I watched a cast of crabs scatter at my feet that I thought of Grandpa again and our visits to Fiddler's Point, and I wondered if I could create people in my stories. I wondered if I recreated Grandpa if he would be the same or only some sort of lesser version of himself. It was something I hesitated to do, but I at least wanted to try.

I spent another few days mulling over recreating Grandpa in my story and planned to do it on a Friday morning. I felt nervous, scared that I wouldn't describe him accurately and would create a flaw that would cheapen my memory of him. I used a photo of Grandpa and me taken one afternoon shortly before he went missing. We'd just gotten back from catching the biggest bass I had ever seen. I'd stood next to Grandpa and, with his help, held up the fish while my father snapped the photo.

I figured it was best to try to capture a moment that meant a lot to me, a moment when I was happy, Grandpa was happy, and I was sure my father felt happy too, capturing the moment through a photograph. We were three men bonding over a fish.

At the writing table, I placed the photo in front of me and opened my notebook.

It was the biggest fish I had ever seen, and practically had to be folded into the large white cooler I helped my grandpa drag back to the house. My father came running out with his camera, and his excitement provoked me to open the cooler and show him our incredible catch. Grandpa laughed at my hasty attempt at flinging the top open to show my father. We all laughed, and my father asked both of us to hold it up so he could take a photo. I grabbed the tail with both hands, and Grandpa grabbed the head and hooked his thumb inside the fish's mouth. Together we raised the fish and smiled for the camera.

I put my pen down and closed my eyes, and when I opened them I saw the white cooler at my feet, but there was neither Grandpa nor my father anywhere around. I tried again, describing Grandpa and my father in more detail.

Grandpa was an old man with thick white hair and a pair of round reading glasses. He wore a bright blue shirt and a pair of khaki shorts. My father stood in front of us, his green-checkered shirt wet around his waist. His camera looped around his neck. He had an infectious grin on his face as he moved the camera to rest slightly on his cheek, ready to take our photo.

Just as before, the cooler was at my feet, and the clothes and camera I had described as worn by Grandpa and my father sat in two piles in the grass. A heavy sadness came over me. Why was I not able to create people? I felt I was so close to seeing Grandpa again in the flesh. The hope that I'd built up over the last few days quickly dissipated. I stared at the photo, wanting it to come to life, but the fish, Grandpa, and my younger self stayed frozen in the picture. The only thing I could produce were tears that rolled down my face. I buried my head in my arms on the writing table.

Through my tears I searched my mind for all the great times I'd spent with Grandpa, and with each memory a new tear added to the pool collecting on the table's surface. I stopped crying when I remembered my last visit with Grandpa, the night he told me about the connection between the squid king and the lonely tree. It was the first time a story came alive to me, and I wondered if it was possible to go to worlds in other books.

I imagined stepping foot on the *Jolly Roger*, drinking tea with the Mad Hatter, or riding a lion named Aslan. I gathered a collection of my favorite books, including *The Lonely Tree*. At the writing table, I pictured myself seeing the chocolate river in *Charlie and the Chocolate Factory*, but nothing happened. I picked up another book and read a few pages. Still nothing. I placed the books at my feet as I went through them, and soon there was but one book left: *The Lonely Tree*.

Since I recalled the night scene by the lake coming to life, it was this page I began reading, and then closed my eyes as tightly as possible. Within a few seconds, the room exploded with light and I was in the story. The budding tulip tree flickered in the wind, and the moonlight bounced off dewy blades of grass. The water moved and shone brightly. Nearby loons echoed through the night, and water lapped the edge of the shore.

This time I took a step toward the lake. I could now move beyond the tulip tree. I followed the sound of the loons and saw them moving in and out of the shadows on the farther end of the lake. I didn't understand how I was able to visit this story and not the others. I walked to the distant end of the lake, thinking of what the missing link could be. I stared at the stars and wanted one to fall with the answer I needed.

My eyes caught lights flickering in the distance, rising above the trees. I didn't recall this in the story, but I walked toward the lights, thinking they would possibly tell me the answer to my question. As I got closer, the sky filled with hundreds of twinkling objects, but they were still a mystery to me. I thought hard and tried to recall my father or someone else reading about the twinkling lights before, but I couldn't remember anyone mentioning them. The closer I got I saw they looked like tiny paper lanterns. They appeared to be coming from just beyond the woods that stood before me.

Although the trek to the other side looked dark and suspicious, my curiosity about the lights pulled me in.

THE LANTERN OF AYLA

Walking through a dark forest by myself and following unknown objects probably wasn't a good idea, but the story of *The Lonely Tree* was so familiar to me that I felt I would be safe from any harm. Through the pine branches overhead, the lights wove in and out of sight. The forest wasn't as dense as I initially thought; about a hundred feet in, I saw an orange glow at the far edge. The closer I got to the other side, the more lights I saw rising from the land.

But about halfway through, a tremendous scream rang through the forest and sent chills up my spine. My internal alarms went off, and I started to run. As I was running, I heard something that sounded like a swarm of bees moving through the trees toward me. My heart leapt into my throat. Though the edge of the forest wasn't far, whatever was behind me was gaining on me. I dashed and hid behind a tree.

Twigs snapped and branches rustled as it swiftly approached and halted a few trees behind me. I covered my mouth to muffle my heavy breathing. Suddenly, in the distance, another loud scream broke through the woods and scared me so much that I fell backward. Afraid I'd been seen, I quickly jumped to my feet and ran as fast as I could toward the edge of the forest where the lights were rising into the sky. In my dash I briefly looked in the direction of the scream and saw two green lights hovering over the ground. They darted in my direction, and I ran even faster.

The buzzing grew louder the closer the green lights got to me, and the hair on the back of my neck stood up. When I reached the edge of the forest, the air was warmer and the buzzing faded and then vanished completely, almost as if the warm air had created a barrier. I kept running until I was far away from the forest, toward a small village. I looked back at the forest to see if I could catch a better glimpse of what had been chasing me. There was nothing but rows and rows of tall, eerie pine trees.

I hunched over and placed my hands on my knees to catch my breath, and then a shrill echoed in my direction and I took off toward the village. At the edge of the town, a wide opening resembling a tunnel spilled its light onto the dirt path. I saw the lights in the sky come from beyond the other side of the tunnel, so I figured the best way to find the origin was to make my way through. The sounds of a busy market got louder as I approached the entrance.

A sign above the tunnel read, "The Grand Bazaar of Ayla City."

I made my way inside and saw exciting throws of color. Rows of mosaic lanterns were strung across the ceiling and illuminated the entire length of the bazaar. The first vendor inside had walls of fabric that rose to the ceiling and altered in shades of magenta, mustard, and tangerine. The vendor on the opposite side sold spices such as saffron, black pepper, oregano, and hot chili labeled by tiny signs that were attached to the wooden bucket that held the spices. Each spice was piled high in the center and looked like a mountain.

The bazaar was busy with people buying all kinds of trinkets and food. Near the center, several booths sold a variety of pistachio-, walnut-, and almond-filled baklava dripping in honey and syrup. The flakes of their fragile, doughy exterior clung to the sign that labeled each version along with its price. The booth opposite sold vibrant-colored fruit such as apples, pears, and apricots, along with a variety of dates and cookies.

Slow rumbling music bounced through the arched ceiling that was painted in yellow and burgundy patterns and had massive windows showing the dark night sky. Every now and then the lights I saw in the sky would quickly pass over the window. I walked by a woman with short, black, curly hair standing in front of a collection of objects.

"Can I interest you in a mug?" she asked.

She pointed to a collection of shiny copper mugs that were strung together and hung from a hook behind her.

I shook my head and said, "No, thank you."

I watched two women go through stacks of jewelry. Rubies, pearls, silver, and gold covered every inch of the counter. Bracelets, rings, and necklaces adorned mirrored trays, their reflection doubling their sparkling attributes.

Children ran up and down the middle of the bazaar chasing one another. A boy who looked about my age ran after a cat, calling it Yishopo as it darted between customers' feet. At one point, the boy almost knocked over a table stacked with plates; the columns of dinnerware swayed back and forth nearly spilling onto the concrete floor. The vendor yelled at the boy, who did not take his eyes off the fleeing cat.

The smell of cloves and cinnamon blanketed the tunnel and seemed to originate from a stand of candles and urns. The burning wicks reflected in the metallic exteriors of the urns and looked as if they were dancing in unison with the music of the bazaar.

At the other end of the market, outside of the tunnel, was a deserted street of shops. There was not a single person on the streets by these stores. I searched the sky for the lights but they appeared to have stopped and only the ones I previously saw were high in the sky. Through the windows in each building, I saw slivers of color, tiny rectangles of red, orange, and blue peeking through the glass.

I approached one of the shops and walked through a set of open double doors. I smelled hints of incense and heard music coming from a cluster of musical instruments by the front door. Upon second glance, I saw the instruments were playing by themselves. The first one that caught my eye was a small, pear-shaped wooden object that looked like a guitar, except the top of the handle was bent backward at a ninety-degree angle.

When I reached out to touch the instrument, a man emerged from in front of me.

"It is an oud. A magical one, of course. Said to have been owned by the Hindu goddess Saraswati," the man said.

The man was small and wore a white turban, green waistcoat, and baggy white pants. I then pointed to the object next to the oud. "Is that a tambourine?"

"That one is called a riq, but yes, it is like a tambourine."

Before I could ask about the third and fourth instruments, the man said, "And that one is a doumbek, which is a goblet-shaped drum made of clay and goat skin. The last one is a mizmar."

I examined the mizmar, which looked like a combination of a flute and a horn. Each one played harmoniously with the others and without the aid of a human.

I turned back to the man and he smiled.

"Greetings, my dear friend."

"Hello," I said.

"Welcome to Babacan's Lantern Shoppe, located in the Bazaar of Ayla City. I am Babacan Talibah, and this is my collection."

He pointed to the array of brightly colored lanterns that hung from every corner of the room. The lanterns looked like the exact ones from the bazaar. From floor to ceiling, glowing ovals and cones of elaborate, colored lights made of broken glass swung from braided strings and black chains. Egg-shaped pendants were plastered with an assortment of radiantly colored mosaic tiles, each one bobbing next to the others like a group of helium-filled balloons.

"My name is Alden. I was walking by and saw your lanterns."

His eyes widened.

"Ah, yes! My Turkish lantern collection is quite exquisite, isn't it?" Babacan marveled at all the lanterns squeezed on top of each other that one might wonder if they were looking at a single lantern or one giant one. "They are quite needed by our people since the blackout."

"Blackout?"

"Ayla City has been in constant darkness for almost three years now, of course!"

"What caused the blackout?"

"No one really knows, but people have their guesses." Babacan walked to the entrance, poked his head out the double doors, and looked up at the sky. "Many people have opinions about how someone stole the sun." He chuckled. "Legends that were once lost now resurface. But perhaps they are just that—lost stories trying to find their way back into the hearts of our people."

I took an extra-long look at the ceiling, since I didn't know what to say.

"But I say the stories have not been lost. Just the people. They stop listening and forget the stories and soon they lose their direction. Direction they would only know by the sun."

"Babacan, how come there is no one at this end of the bazaar?"

"This is the Lantern District, a long row of shops that sell the illuminating lamps you see before you." He pointed to the wall of bobbing lanterns behind me.

"You see, we are responsible for lighting the lanterns you may have seen in the sky," he said.

"Yes, I did see them! They are what brought me here."

Babacan smiled and clasped his hands together with joy.

"Then they have done their job, haven't they?" he asked.

I looked at him with slight confusion. "Is that how you attract customers?"

"Well—one particular customer," Babacan responded.

I still did not understand, but Babacan continued as he pointed to the sky.

Just then a young boy entered the shop and said, "Babacan we need a few more lanterns before we call it a night."

Without even looking at the boy, Babacan responded, "There is no need. The boy for which we light the lanterns for has arrived and he is standing right here. The lanterns are for you Alden."

The boy exited the shop, and through the open doors, I saw hundreds of mosaic lanterns rise from between the two buildings down the street. More lanterns appeared, and then people emerged from the side roads, carrying lanterns and releasing them into the sky.

I walked out onto the street as the lanterns took flight. Men, women, and children of all ages and dressed in colorful garments greeted one another with their lanterns and then released them into the darkness above. The lanterns were the twinkling lights I saw beyond the forest.

"What do you mean they release them just for me?" I asked.

Babacan's eyes deepened, and he pointed to the sky.

The lanterns that were first released were far and high in the sky, and as soon as Babacan pointed to the sky, the lanterns exploded like an exciting show of fireworks. As each cluster of lanterns reached the same altitude they too exploded into a shower of color.

"They release the lanterns once a year, to let our loved ones who have passed into the heavens know we are still here, but for the last three years, they have done so every night—to bring a young boy named Alden to Ayla City."

"Me? For what?"

"To save us from the darkness."

Tears ran down his face. He quickly grasped my hands and plunked down on the front steps of his shop. I had no choice but to sit down with him.

"Your grandfather was a dear friend of mine—"

"You knew Grandpa?"

"Yes, in fact, I met him when I was probably your age. We spent a lot of time during the summers together, and as we got older, his visits became less frequent, but he made sure to come at least once a year."

I stared at Babacan and tried to make sense of what he was saying.

"Colvin was an extraordinary man with an extraordinary gift for writing, and I assume he sent you here to help us."

"Grandpa didn't send me. I saw the lanterns and followed them through the forest."

"Well, Colvin told me that, should he not return, he would send his grandson—you."

"Grandpa disappeared almost three years ago. Babacan, we need to back up for a minute. How do you know Grandpa?"

Babacan stood up and motioned for me to follow him back inside his shop. The colored lanterns floated along the walls, wanting to be released like the questions in my head.

We settled at a tiny table behind the cash register. Babacan pulled two teacups from a cupboard and placed them on the table. Then he grabbed a steaming kettle and dispensed a dark liquid, which I presumed was tea or coffee. After my cup was full to the top, he poured a cup for himself. This time, the liquid was red.

"How did you do that?"

"One of your grandfather's inventions. It's a teakettle that dispenses the type of tea your taste buds prefer the most. Mine, of course, is raspberry tea with one sugar, and yours appears to be black tea. How does it taste?"

It had hints of jasmine that reminded me of the yellow jasmine that grew around Grandpa's pool. It had just the right amount of sweetness too.

"It's…very good actually," I said.

Babacan got up and retrieved a plate from the counter stacked with mini-cakes the size of doughnuts, each one a different color and displayed on the platter looking like a painter's pallet.

"Turkish cakes, or as we sometimes call it here, Ayla apps, since they are mainly used as an appetizer and only made in our city. Notice how they're the same colors as my lanterns? My wife makes them. Well, go on. Try one. They go well with the tea."

I picked up a red one dusted with pink sugar and red sprinkles. As I took a bite, a sudden rush of happiness hit me.

"Strawberry Fields always brings joy to me too!" he said.

Babacan picked a green one.

"Hmm, Key Lime," he said.

My elation quickly diminished, and I thought of Grandpa again.

"Babacan, my grandpa?"

He placed his cake on the table and dabbed his mouth with a napkin.

"Yes, yes, please allow me to tell you all I know," he said.

I placed my half-eaten cake on the table and scooted my chair closer.

"As I said earlier, I met your grandfather when I was around your age. He would tell me about his city, and I would tell him about mine. Your grandfather had a way of making me forget all of my troubles. In fact, I do not remember a single thing about my life until I met Colvin. We would go fishing, build forts in the forest, eat ice cream by the lake, and swap stories of each other's worlds."

Babacan had a faraway look, and I could tell he was reliving those days with Grandpa.

"He would come often, but as he got older his visits became shorter and shorter, and when we became adults with families, he came only once a year. Then one day a few years ago—shortly after our world went dark—he said he was close to finding out what happened to the pendulum in the Time Table."

"What pendulum, and what is the Time Table?"

I felt myself falling further down the rabbit hole and my questions stacking up.

"The Time Table is a place that tracks time for every story ever written. When a writer begins his or her story, it's registered with the Grandfather Clock, a majestic clock that resides in the middle of the city. The pendulum rests within the clock, and it's what logs time."

"And what happened to it?"

"Your grandfather said the pendulum was stolen, which caused all these time shifts and sent our city into darkness."

The barrage of new information made me wonder what kind of secret life Grandpa had lived.

"Did all places go into darkness?" I asked.

"No. But we heard of varying degrees of time shifts from neighboring towns and travelers on their way to the Time Table. A woman from a place called Brighton said her town was in constant daylight. It never got darker than a midday afternoon. It all seemed so simple at first—"

"At first?" I asked with concern.

"Then people started dying, dropping dead in the street. Most just collapsed, but some started aging faster and faster, until they died quite before their time. No one understood it until those travelers started reporting the same occurrences. Whoever stole the pendulum set off a catastrophic chain of events that disrupted our world and killed our people."

The severity of the situation sank in. I realized the dire state Babacan's people were in.

"And you said your townspeople were sending the lanterns in the sky for me?"

"During your grandfather's last visit, he mentioned that he thought he knew where the stolen pendulum was, and if he did not return the following day, then I should make sure we released the lanterns every night until you arrived."

Babacan then pulled a small leather notebook that was no bigger than the palm of his hand and wrapped in thick black rope from his pocket and held it out to me.

"He also told me to give this to you. When our people started dying, I tried to open it in hope of finding something that might help, but it's wrapped in rope that cannot be broken or unwound."

The rope felt rough in my hands as I took the notebook.

"He did not tell me anything else. I hope you forgive me for trying to open what was not mine. To see those you know and love die—"

"Babacan, you don't have to explain. I would have done the same thing."

"Thank you."

I looked back down and further examined the notebook.

"This all sounds crazy to me," I said. "I'm just a boy who discovered I could go to the places I write about. Did Grandpa think I could help in some way?"

"I can't say for certain, but perhaps the answers are in that book. Do you know how to untie it?"

"No clue," I said as I tried to pull the rope apart from both the front and back.

Babacan had given me so much—yet so little. Nothing made sense.

I placed the notebook on the table in front of me and wondered if accepting ownership of the notebook was also accepting to help fix the shift in time.

As I stood up, Babacan fell to his knees and grabbed my hands.

"Alden, you must help us! Please help us! I don't know what else to do!" he pleaded. His face was panicked.

I had never felt as needed as I did at that moment.

"You must think about what it would be like to lose your loved ones. Your family and friends dying without a moment's notice."

I did know what it felt like. Grandpa was with me one day and then gone the next. I tried to imagine if my father and mother had vanished too. I probably would be on my knees like Babacan, desperate enough to beg an unknown child for help.

Babacan wiped away his tears.

"I have something else for you," he said.

He held out his hand, his palm to the ceiling, and abruptly three men appeared on a balcony inside the shop, standing in a horizontal line. The men wore similar clothing as Babacan, except their turbans each had a different color. I examined the man with a bright red turban, who stood on the far right. Like the others, his face was concealed in a shadow and he wielded a sheath by his side.

As if they were given a perfectly timed instruction, each man grabbed the grip of his sword and in unison pulled the blade halfway out of its sheath. At the same time, a large glowing lantern with mosaic tiles in the shape of a sunburst descended into Babacan's hand. The middle sunburst was bright yellow, followed by a larger one that was red, then purple, then green, then orange, and finally blue. It was magnificent.

"This is the Lantern of Ayla," Babacan said. "It is our city's most precious possession. It contains the light of our people. Thousands upon thousands of happy thoughts and memories of everyone living in the city are what fuels this lantern's light. After the blackout, it was decided among the city officials to grant this lantern to you, as we believed that if Colvin, a dear friend of ours, was to put all his faith in you, then it would be our duty to provide you with a piece of the city to help you on your journey to restore the time shift. Take this lantern with you. When you need to light your path, just lean over the lantern and whisper, 'Ayla.' The lantern will illuminate your way."

"Thank you," I said.

The lantern drifted away from Babacan's palm and shrunk to the size of a lemon so it fit into a cloth bag. He handed the bag to me along with Grandpa's notebook from the table.

"Babacan, I don't know about all this. I don't know what Grandpa was thinking when he told you I could help."

"There is a spectacular light within you, and there is no limit to how bright it can shine," he said as he hugged me.

We walked together toward the shop door and out onto the street. I left with a heavy heart and the burden of saving a city from oblivion. My place of escape had become the place I needed to escape from.

As I walked back through the bazaar, I paid less attention to the merchandise and more to the vendors, their families, and their livelihood that brought light to what would otherwise be a dark, lifeless tunnel. I watched as a mother swaddled her crying baby in a blue flowing garment, a boy and his younger sister begged their dad for some money for a bag of sweets, and an old woman solemnly organized her table of clay pots. It would be shameful not to help Babacan and his people.

As I approached the field, I realized I had forgotten about the buzzing and the horrific screaming that had chased me through the woods. The memorable bazaar made me forget about the frightening green eyes that mysteriously disappeared after I made it out of the forest.

But there appeared to be no way back except through the forest. Before entering it again, I listened for any sign of movement, but it was quiet. The forest seemed darker and more haunting than before. Perhaps it was just my knowing of what may be hiding within the maze of trees that made me more fearful about my reentry. There was no point in waiting until morning; I knew there would be no morning. This place was in perpetual darkness—a darkness I was supposed to fix.

I decided not to use the lantern Babacan had given me. I didn't want to attract whatever was chasing me before, but with every step, pine needles and branches rustled and cracked. I started to feel delirious as I wound my way through complete darkness.

After a while, I decided to take out the lantern Babacan gave me, figuring that whatever was tracking me would be tipped off already from the noise I was making stumbling through the woods. If I had light, I would probably make it back more quickly.

I opened the bag, grabbed the lantern, and whispered, "Ayla." The lantern spun in place, and a light gradually emanated from within. The lantern then flew into the air above my head and grew larger before it exploded with light. Sparks burst from the sunburst pattern, and I held my hands over my head, sure the explosion would send branches on top of me. The explosion was only temporary, and once the last sparks had fallen, the lantern hovered overhead and glowed with a bright golden light. My eyes adjusted, and I saw everything around me. Branches were strewn everywhere, and huge caves with dirt mounds piled outside of them were directly in front of me. I probably would have walked right into one. There must have been a dozen of them, but I didn't recall seeing them before. I felt cold air billowing out from their dark holes. Did whatever was following me live in these caves? I wasn't going to stay and find out.

I ran as fast as I could, with Babacan's lantern leading the way. I made it back to the writing table, and just as I sat down, the lantern flew to my side and flickered before shrinking back to its original size. I held out my hand and the lantern gently landed in my palm before I placed it back in the bag and into my pocket.

When I looked up, I saw a pair of green eyes glowing at the edge of the woods, and I heard the distinct buzzing sound and a scream. I immediately thought of home.

GRANDPA ROWE

My eyes adjusted from the darkness of Ayla City to the bright, sunlit loft. I thought of Babacan and my new responsibility. It haunted me. Where would I be if I didn't have my parents? I thought about my father, who was constantly sick and most recently had developed an unexpected lump in one of his legs. What if he was gone?

I thought about the young parents in Ayla City who were taken by the time change and left their children behind. It was the young who seemed most cheated.

I imagined birthdays, graduations, weddings, and all of life's grand events pilfered from Babacan's people. I thought of my own life events that Grandpa had already missed: learning to write in cursive, memorizing multiplication tables, turning nine and ten, and more extraordinary, discovering my ability to travel to the stories I wrote about.

My life began to feel small. Ayla City was, in some respects, fictional, but the people and places seemed as real as the teachers at my school, the baker at the grocery store, and the dentist who cleaned my teeth. The more I stood there, the more it sunk in. I would have to commit to helping Babacan, and then maybe I'd find out what happened to Grandpa.

I reached in my pocket, where before returning to the loft I'd shoved the Lantern of Ayla. Grandpa's notebook was in my right pocket, but the lantern was missing. I looked under the writing table and around my chair to see if it had fallen out, but I couldn't find it. I thought it must have fallen out, but I was too afraid to go back to the woods to look for it.

I walked over to the window and saw my parents' cars in the driveway. They usually came home much later, so that was odd. I wondered if they had discovered yet that I was missing school, so I tried to think of an excuse to soften the truth. I thought of telling them I was afraid to go to class because of a kid who picked on me. It was plausible, since they knew I'd been picked on in the past. Maybe I would tell them I kept forgetting my books, so each day I came home to get them, but it always took hours to find where I last put them, so there was no point in going back. And even if I did try to go back, I would have to wait for the city bus.

I knew that would never work, so I decided I would tell them the truth—that I spent my days writing stories and used Grandpa's magical writing table to visit fictional worlds. It occurred to me that that sounded more bizarre than the previous excuse. They would surely up my medication, and I would have to spend even more time with my psychiatrist, taking away my time to find out what happened to Grandpa and save cities of people. *I could save cities of people*, I thought.

Not really knowing which excuse I was going to go with, I made my way toward the house, tucking the notebook back inside my pocket.

When I entered the house, my parents were sitting next to each other on the couch, and my mother had her arms around my father. Tears streaked down her face and shimmered in the sunlight that came through a nearby window. She motioned for me to sit. By her quick glance at my father, I could tell they were about to give me some serious news that had nothing to do with me missing school.

"Honey come sit down with us," my mother said.

My parents scooted down the sofa to make room for me. I sat next to my mother and she grabbed my hand.

"We met with some doctors this morning," my mother said. She glanced at my father and then turned her attention back to me. "The lump in your father's leg is a rare type of cancer and has spread to his lungs." Tears swelled in her eyes.

My father squeezed her hand and said rather plainly, "There is no sense in getting upset. The doctors have outlined a plan to treat the spots they found in my lungs, so there's nothing to worry about. They said they can also remove the cancer in my leg and treat it with radiation."

My life was playing out like some after-school special: the parents sitting next to the child, trying to comfort him as they unleash terrible news of the C-word. I reacted just as any child would: I cried along with my mother.

They told me dates of appointments and treatments, but they felt like stepping-stones to a road of pain and grief. I knew how most of the after-school specials ended, but my father's cavalier reaction gave me hope that maybe we could beat this.

After we all calmed down, I noticed several boxes labeled "ROWE" near the front door.

"What are those?" I asked through the wad of tissue I held to my nose.

"Boxes from the university. Grandpa's things from his office," my mother said. "I was cleaning out the hall closet and found them. I had forgotten I put them there. Perhaps they will fit in the loft."

I got up and walked over to the three boxes and pushed them to the center of the room. I knelt down to open one, and my parents joined me. We opened the boxes as if it was Christmas morning, each one the perfect distraction from the news of my father's cancer.

Each was filled to the top with various items: pencils, pens, name-plates, awards, plaques, pictures. My mother pulled a photograph of me as a child with Grandpa from the clutter. She held it up.

"It looks like you with Dad at a book signing," my father said. "I don't remember you attending a book signing of his. I wonder who took the picture."

"Why is Grandpa signing those books? Did he contribute a piece to it?" I asked.

My parents looked at each other as if expecting the other to answer my question.

"You know, I don't know. I don't remember this either," my mother said with confusion.

"Perhaps this was a signing for his book?" my father said as he held the picture closer to his face and examined the photo in more detail.

My father's eyes squinted and examined the section of the picture where a stack of books sat at the end of the table.

"The cover looks like his book, so it must have been an event when it was first published," my father said.

"I didn't know Grandpa published a book!"

"What? Yes, you did. You made us read you his book every night." My mother laughed.

"What book?" I asked.

My parents exchanged a look.

"*The Lonely Tree*! How do you not remember that book? Didn't I see you with it just the other day?" my mother asked.

The wheels started turning. I was able to travel to the story in *The Lonely Tree* but not to any other—

"But that book was written by—"

And at the same time, my father and I said, "Cal Caulder."

"Grandpa's pen name. I thought we told you all this," my father added.

All these years of listening to Grandpa read that story and I never knew he was the person who had written it. I wondered if it pleased him that I always asked him to read *The Lonely Tree* when I stayed over during the summer. Memories of his slicked-back hair, white V-neck shirts, and khaki shorts swept over me as if it were just yesterday.

I recalled some nights he would fix me vanilla ice cream with chocolate syrup, and then afterward chase me down the hall, where I would fly into bed and wait for him to read me the story.

These were memories I cherished, although my childhood memories seemed limited. Perhaps it was only natural to remember a handful of memories from childhood.

I thought of how some of Babacan's people would never get to have such memories. And then a piece of the puzzle came together: the story that led me to Babacan was the story Grandpa wrote. This victory was short-lived, however, and replaced with another question: the lights, the forest, and Ayla City were never in the story, so how was I able to see and visit those places?

My mother handed me the photograph, and I studied it. I was very young and smiling as I sat next to Grandpa, a green blanket and pacifier in my hands. I examined our faces and the blurred scene behind us. It was then I noticed two unusual things: the upper right corner of the picture looked smudged, as if someone's finger had smeared the ink. It gave the illusion the photo was hand painted and the painter accidentally smudged the paint near the edge. I always thought photos were developed by a machine, so the chance of the ink smearing from human intervention was almost nonexistent. I wondered if the picture was even real or if it was painted.

I examined our faces and the blurred scene behind us. Only then did I see Grandpa holding the rope-bound journal under his left arm.

I held the photo out to my parents and asked if they ever saw Grandpa with that notebook. I pulled the notebook Babacan gave me from my pocket and showed them how it matched the one in the picture.

"It looks just like this one, doesn't it?" I asked.

"It sure looks like the same one," my father said. "I can't recall ever seeing him with it, do you, Kay?"

He handed the photo to my mother with one hand and held out his other for me to give him the notebook.

"I've never seen him with such a notebook. How did you come across it?" my mother asked.

I thought about telling them the truth—the writing table, the field, the woods, Babacan, all of it—but thoughts of more meds stopped me.

"I found it in the loft, in Grandpa's writing table," I said.

"That writing table is so odd looking. Where did he say he got that thing, Jay?" my mother asked.

My father turned the notebook over in his hands.

"You know, I'm not sure. I don't think he ever told me. Alden, you have this rope on here too tight. I can't get it off," he said.

"I didn't put the rope on there. I found it that way, and I haven't figured out how to get it off either."

"Grab one of the knives from the kitchen. I bet we can cut it off," my mother suggested.

I fetched the sharpest knife in the kitchen.

"Try this one," I said.

My father took the knife and tried to slide it across the rope, but with a swift movement the knife glided across the notebook, flew across the room, and lodged itself in the wall.

My mother gasped. "That almost hit Alden!"

"What the…!" my father shouted.

I walked over, pulled the knife out of the wall, and handed it back to my father.

"Try again," I said.

"No way! That thing almost killed you! Now get over here away from that knife!" my mother said.

"Let's try and burn it off," my father suggested.

My mother pleaded for me to stop as I ran to grab a lighter from a kitchen drawer.

"You'll light the whole thing on fire and burn our house down with it!" my mom said.

My father was a little more daring, so I knew he would not object to at least trying to burn the rope.

"Alden, grab a large saucepan so if it does catch on fire we have something to put it on that won't catch the house on fire," my father said.

I handed my father the saucepan and lighter. He held the book out in front of him and pressed his finger on the lighter switch. We watched as the rope repelled the flame. The flame from the lighter simply would not touch the rope. Instead, the flame split as if it was wrapping itself around an invisible shield covering the rope.

"Well darn!" my father said, putting the lighter down. He tossed the notebook to me and said, "Better hold on to it for a bit and don't try cutting it open with anything sharp!"

"What about my wall?" my mother said.

"I'll grab some putty from the loft, and we will patch it up. I'll go to the store this weekend and get them to match the paint on the wall. It will be just as new," my father said.

My father picked up two boxes and said to me, "Now help me take these boxes to the loft."

I picked up the third box, and we carried them to the loft while my mother stayed behind and stared at the hole in the wall.

Once we were up in the loft, we stacked the boxes against the back wall. "I've got some hedge clippers up here somewhere. What do you say we give those a try?" my father asked me.

My eyes caught the bright blue handles of the clippers propped up in a corner. "Here they are!"

My father wedged the clippers under the rope and squeezed the handles together. He squeezed as hard as he could to the point his face turned beet red and the veins in his forehead could be seen.

"Dad, just stop. You're going to kill yourself."

He finally stopped and took a few short breaths.

"That rope must be coated in cement. It's impossible to get it off," my father said. He picked up the notebook and handed it to me. "Just be careful with it. Promise me you won't try and remove it by yourself. If anything happens to you, your mother will kill me."

I thought what else could I possibly try to remove the rope with. After seeing it deflect the knife into the wall, there was no way I was going to try and cut it off on my own.

"I'm going back into the house," my father said. Before my father left, I hugged him tighter than I'd ever hugged anyone before. It was a conscious hug, where I took in every part of that moment: the smell of my father's cologne, the strength of his arms, his heartbeat, his breathing.

"We will beat this, Dad. Don't you worry."

He smiled and then sneezed. "It's just a rope," he said.

"I'm talking about the cancer."

"Thanks, Alden. I'm glad you're up for the challenge."

"Dad, you've got a little…"

He removed a tissue from his pocket and wiped his nose.

"Looks like I picked up another cold."

My father then noticed the writing table and walked over to it. He sat down in front of it, ran his hands over the top, and tried to pull out some of the drawers. He passed his fingers over the front legs and around the outline of the clock. His eyes were far away, and it felt as if he was greeting an old friend.

"Did you ever use this table when you were a kid?" I asked him.

I hoped that he answered in a way that would let me know if he too knew of the table's secret power.

"I…can't remember. I guess I'm just getting old. It seems I haven't been able to answer any of your questions lately."

"You don't remember anything about where this table came from? It looks pretty unique. Not something you would see in a department store," I said.

My father paused and repeated his examination of the table.

"I don't. I'm sorry. Fascinating, though, isn't it? It looks like one of a kind. These front legs look like horns from some animal."

"I thought so too. Maybe the horns of a couple of rhinos?"

"Your grandpa did love to write at it, though," my father said. "It seemed like every time I stopped by to visit, he was anxiously writing away at this table. Writing like he was on a hurried mission to save the world."

I wondered if my father knew about the table's magic ability, so I pressed the topic.

"Have you written anything at this table *recently*?" I asked.

"No, I don't think so. Writing is your grandpa's thing. I'm the paint-er. I don't think he even allowed anyone else to sit at this table. In fact, I don't think I've ever been alone with it before. From what I can remember, any time I stopped by and Grandpa wasn't home, the door to his office where the table sat was always closed. That or he was sitting at it."

I imagined Grandpa was off in one of his stories whenever the door was closed, but I found it odd my father couldn't recall any history about the table or think of a time when he'd sat at the table by himself.

"Oh well, I'll let you know if anything comes to mind," he said.

He placed his arm around me, and we made our way to the stairs, but my curiosity begged me to look further into Grandpa's boxes.

"Dad, is it okay if I take a few minutes up here and finish a home-work assignment for Mr. Brevard?"

"Sure, I'll call you when dinner is ready."

As soon as I heard him close the door, I began to process the con-tents of the boxes with the intent of finding some link to Grandpa's disappearance—and the time shift. I hoped I would find some magical cure for my father's cancer at the same time.

The first box contained typical office supplies: stapler, tape dispens-er, thumbtacks, sticky notes, and the like. The second box, the box my mother had opened, held more personal items: a coffee mug with "World's #1 Dad" on it and awards Grandpa received from the universi-ty. One award read: "Faculty Member of the Year." Another: "The Award for Outstanding Creative Writing." The gold plates were scratched from loose objects in the box.

Grandpa was responsible, hardworking, and accomplished, but the more I discovered, the more I realized how little I knew about him.

Grandpa led a complicated and adventurous life, in the real world and in his stories. He had been on a quest to uncover a grand mystery, to single-handedly help cities of people, and I was in awe of that mission.

The third box, the one my father had opened, contained teaching manuals and textbooks. I took each one out and flipped through its pages, hoping something would catch my attention. After looking through two large textbooks and three thinner teaching manuals, I came across a book: a small black metal journal with an embossed clock on the cover.

THE TIME TABLE

The metal journal I found at the bottom of the box had to have something to do with the Time Table that Babacan had told me about. I opened it and was excited to read the first entry, titled "The Time Table." The text described a clock-themed world where clocks were used in every aspect of the city. The entry was filled with descriptions of clock gears used as escalators, bridges in various forms of the minute and hour hands, and cars and boats in the shapes of numbers with horns that mimicked different alarm clock tones.

I placed the metal journal on the writing table, and with the rope-bound journal in my pocket, I closed my eyes and watched the image of the Time Table come alive.

When I opened my eyes, Grandpa's metal journal was no longer in front of me and in its place was the Lantern of Ayla. The placement was in the exact location of where the metal journal had sat, as if the journal had magically transformed into the lantern. I placed the lantern in my pocket and saw I was in an alley between two large buildings.

Before I stood up, I noticed the clock in the middle of the writing table was glowing and rotating in place, inching out from the round hole it rested in. The clock squeaked as it twisted from its holding cell, and it eventually popped out into my hand. The clock felt heavy, like a sock full of quarters. I turned it over and saw the clock hands spinning continuously every which way.

The outer coating was scratched and tarnished like an old penny, giving it an aged look. A skinny chain was attached around a copper loop in the back. Beneath the loop was text that looked like calligraphy and burned amber red:

Time is mastered in a series of four
with each taking dichotomy explored.
If you are wise the Guards will see
collecting them all will set us free.

I repeated the words and wondered what they meant. Perhaps it was another clue Grandpa left behind. I tried to recall ever seeing the clock missing from the table or a moment when he might have carried it around. I held the chain as the clock dangled and spun in the air. It now looked like a traditional pocket watch.

The alley was dark and deserted. Up ahead, in front of the buildings, people walked by and the light moved from dark to bright in rapid succession. I made my way through the alley, mesmerized by the quick shifting of light above.

THE TIME TABLE

Once out of the alley, I saw I was standing on the outer edge of a circular courtyard that resembled a replica of my pocket watch, with the exception of the dial, which was gold. Overhead, the sun moved with the hands of the clock, which sat beneath a glass floor that extended from the center of the courtyard to the front doors of the surrounding buildings. When the sun faded, the moon rose from the opposite direction. In a matter of minutes, the sun had set and the moon had risen at least a dozen times.

Time constantly moved in this place. All around me were tall buildings that stretched high into the sky, each one a different shape. The building to my right was triangular, with one side shorter than the other. The sides were made of tiny alarm clocks stacked on top of one another. All of the clocks looked alike, their hands stuck at seven o'clock.

To my left was a short, circular building that connected with another building of similar size and shape. They almost looked like two circles sitting next to each other.

I watched as herds of people scurried into the buildings, but none of them had as much action as the two buildings across from me. They sat within a few feet of each other but did not appear to connect. The building on the right was wide and curved in the middle, where people were entering a small door. The building on the left was taller than all the other buildings surrounding the courtyard and looked like a traditional skyscraper. It was the busiest building.

The people who came in and out wore suits and ties and dressed liked they worked on Wall Street. Each person examined a clock attached to his or her jacket every few minutes. One woman stopped, looked at her watch, and then darted into the short, wide building, as if she was late for something.

All around the courtyard people were sitting on benches, eating and talking. There were light posts by each bench, and every time the sun disappeared, the lights would come on, and then shut off again when the sun rose.

The people seemed unfazed by the quick changing of time. They continued with their daily business as if nothing were out of the ordinary. I walked a little ways and continued to examine the city block. I made my way to the tall skyscraper, and when I reached its entrance, I noticed a sign in front that read, "Time is Money."

I sat down on one of the nearby benches and watched people go in and out, and I wondered what was attracting everyone inside. The action was constant. A few people casually walked inside, but the majority of the people ran through the doors almost in a panic, as if their lives depended on getting inside at a specific time. The only common theme was that everyone had a pocket watch and pulled it out to check the time when they passed by the building.

From my own pocket I removed the watch that fell out of the writing table. The hands continued to spin erratically. When I looked up, my eyes went back to the alley I first emerged from, and then I noticed a woman walking directly toward me from the center of the courtyard. She was not dressed like the others. She wore a khaki button-down shirt and matching khaki shorts with a set of tools that dangled from her belt and large, heavy-duty boots. She looked like someone about to go on an African safari. On top of her thick Afro, she wore a pair of goggles that looked like two large magnifying glasses. When she was within a few feet of me, she held out her hand and said, "Hello. Welcome to the Time Table."

"Hello. My name is—"

"Alden Rowe. Yes, I know."

"How?" I stopped her before she could answer me. "Wait, do you know Grandpa?"

"Yes, my name is Tula, and your grandpa was a close friend of mine."

"He wrote about this place in a book back home."

"I'm sure he did. This is where stories begin and end. Our city is constantly monitoring the timelines of all stories throughout the world. Once a time of day has been established in a story, it's registered in this building right here." She pointed to the skyscraper.

"So every story ever written is logged in that building?" I asked.

"Yes."

I realized the building was the place Babacan told me about. "That's amazing!"

"Even the fairy tales read to me as a child? All the stories written by famous authors like Hans Christian Andersen and the Brothers Grimm? Their stories' timelines are logged in this building?"

"Yes!" she exclaimed. "Now, come on, let's load your watch."

"Load my watch?"

"Yes, of course. That is *your* watch there in your hands, is it not?"

I looked down at the pocket watch and presented it to her.

Not really looking at it, she took the watch in her hand and said, "Great, now follow me."

She led me toward the large doors at the center of the skyscraper. The building had a grand lobby completely made of glass. The floor was glass, the walls were glass, and even the security desk at the front was made of glass. Beyond the security desk in a second promenade sat three large letters, PPF, with a slogan at the bottom that read, "Your Past, Present, and Future." The second *P* was taller than the first, and the *F* was the tallest of the three. Pressed right next to the *F* was a towering, skinny grandfather clock made of thick glass that resembled an ice sculpture. It rose all the way to the building's ceiling.

Unlike a traditional pendulum that swung back and forth, in this clock the pendulum spun very quickly in the base. It spun so fast that all one could really see were beams of silver light twisting inside the glass case. Where the rod would normally connect to the pendulum, a solid beam of white light ran straight down the center. The clock's hands and face were made of glass. The whole thing was opulent and hypnotic.

"Now, come with me so we can get some more time on that watch," she said, holding her arm out toward me. I followed her down a corridor and we passed through a narrow doorway.

"I met your grandfather many years ago. I am his timekeeper," Tula said.

"What is a timekeeper?"

"I'll get to all that in a bit, but we must hurry," she said.

We continued to the end of the hallway, through a set of glass doors with clock hands as handles. Inside were several rows of clocks resembling giant pods, each occupied by a person. Men and women were lined up in front of the pods. When they got to the front of the line, they presented their watch to the person inside.

"What are these people doing with their watches?" I asked Tula. We were next in line.

"This is the time bank. Everyone comes here to fill their watches with time. We need to fill your watch with time before it runs out," she said.

We stepped up to the pod. She quickly handed the watch to an old man dressed in a pin-striped suit and top hat. He looked like how I imagined the president of a bank would dress. His thick white hair protruded from under his hat, and he had a full white mustache that shimmered. Tula placed the watch in his white-gloved palm, and he looked at it with intense curiosity, flipping it over several times.

"This looks like a very old watch, and it's strange the way the hands are spinning," he said.

He placed the watch in a box, and it glowed silver and then gold. The man was astonished by the strange glow and stumbled backward. He looked around to his colleagues, who had also been distracted by the glowing sequence.

"How spectacular!" the man behind us exclaimed.

Even Tula was enraptured by the unique result.

The man opened the box, and with a puzzled look he held the watch close to his ear. He then examined the face of the watch and shook it.

"That's strange. It didn't load any time. Let me try it again," he said.

Just as before, the box glowed silver and then transitioned to gold. The clock didn't load. He handed the watch to a man who entered the pod from behind him. The second man tried. Yet again they were unable to fill the watch with time.

"Oh dear. We'd better call Mr. Zolaky over," said the second man.

A crowd of spectators had gathered around the pod. The second man pressed a black button on the top right of the counter. Almost

71

immediately, a slender man with shoulder-length salt-and-pepper hair joined the now-crowded pod.

"What seems to be the problem now, Frank?" he said curtly, rolling his eyes.

Frank explained what had happened. Mr. Zolaky sighed and tried it himself. When the problem persisted, he appeared untroubled.

"Sorry, but this watch is defective. We seem to have such problems with these older models, and unfortunately there's nothing we can do. I can't even tell you how much time you have left," he said, a vacant expression on his face. He looked at the clock one last time and shook it in the air as if he were trying to quickly fling a bug off the back of his hand. The hands stopped for a brief moment. "It looks like you only have a minute left," he said. The hands then began spinning fitfully again. Mr. Zolaky handed the watch back to me.

The crowd watched with alarmed expressions on their faces; some even gasped and cupped their mouths in trepidation.

"What happens when my time runs out?" I asked Tula.

She stumbled over her words. "Uh...uh...um."

Tula looked to the crowd for an answer.

"Tula, what's going to happen?" I persisted.

All she could do was stare in shock. The crowd anxiously shuffled, and more people looked at their watches and then back at me. Finally, one man shouted, "It's been a minute already."

Another minute went by.

"It's been two minutes and nothing is happening!" shouted a woman.

"What kind of a prank is this?" asked another woman.

As the minutes ticked, the crowd disbanded and people went about their daily routines. The men in the pods continued filling watches with time. Tula and I stood motionless in a sea of people.

She then grabbed my hand and led me back down the corridor into the lobby with the glass Grandfather Clock. We exited the building and stopped in the courtyard.

"Tula, why wouldn't my watch—"

"Let me see it again," she said.

I handed her the watch. She ran her finger over the face, examined the back, and shook it just as the men had done.

"Well? What are you looking for?" I asked.

"Are you sure this is *your* watch?"

"Well, no, this is the watch that fell out of the writing table."

"There must be another watch where you entered. Maybe you just didn't see it. Let's go look."

The writing table remained hidden in the alley. We searched all around and tried opening all the drawers again, but they were all still sealed shut. There was no other watch.

"The watch fell out of this hole by itself when I first arrived here," I said as I moved my finger around the empty hole.

"This is your grandfather's writing table, right?" Tula asked as she ran her fingers over the top of the writing table.

"Yes, why?"

Instead of answering my question, she inspected every corner of the desk. I felt like she knew more about the watch and the writing table than she was letting on.

"What is it?" I asked.

"Follow me," she said.

I nodded and walked with her to the building with the triangular shape. A round green clock functioned as the entrance to the building. The large hands on the door didn't move. The short hand pointed at the seven, and the long one pointed at the six. It was seven thirty. In the middle of the hands was the symbol of a crown, the kind that adorned a king's head. I watched it glow as we entered the building.

As soon as we walked inside, I could tell it was a restaurant by all the booths filled with people eating food. The familiar smells of bacon and coffee wafted toward me, and the sounds of dishes clanking mingled with the many people scraping their plates and slurping their drinks.

One side of the restaurant appeared to be serving dinner, as hearty stews and large helpings of chicken and mashed potatoes steamed on a buffet near the front door. On the other side, teacups and coffee mugs littered the tables. A waitress served pancakes to a couple in a booth near a window. Another couple read a newspaper, circling sections, while they ate bacon and eggs.

What an extraordinary concept. The side eating dinner sat in dim candlelight, and the side eating breakfast basked in a sunny view of the city. Each side was also decorated according to the time of day. The dinner side was designed using warm, neutral colors that when combined with the dim light made the space smolder like a nighttime fire. Rich tones of burgundy, gold, and emerald green were cast upon the walls by various pictures, art, and sconces.

The breakfast side was decorated with bright yellows, whites, and blues. The tablecloths were a checkered blue and yellow and gave the impression one was sitting at a farmhouse breakfast nook.

74

"What is this place?" I asked Tula.

"This is the Timer Diner. They serve dinner and breakfast all day. You may have noticed the time on the exterior. Seven thirty, but no a.m. or p.m. Perfect time—either way—for breakfast or dinner."

A host asked if we were eating dinner or breakfast.

"Which do you prefer?" Tula asked.

"Well, I have to admit I've lost track of time, so I have no idea what time of day it actually is, but I much prefer breakfast to dinner any day," I said.

"Breakfast it is, then," Tula said to the host.

We followed the host to a corner booth. It was nice and private, which made me feel very comfortable. The host placed a menu in front of each of us. I opened it to see what was being served. Everything sounded incredible. The menu included all the normal breakfast staples: French toast with fruit, scrambled eggs, stacks of pancakes, every omelet combination possible, and at least twenty different tea and coffee options.

I decided on some pumpkin pancakes but didn't see any prices—where prices should appear, there were only clocks with bars going through them. Some had two bars, some had four, and so on.

"What do the little clocks mean?" I asked.

"Oh, that's the cost of your meal."

"What do you mean?"

"You pay with time—the time from your pocket watch. But since you mysteriously don't have any time on your watch, I'll pay for us."

"Thank you."

A server took our order, then held out a box like the one the man had at the time bank. Tula handed her the watch, the server closed the box, and after it illuminated, she removed the watch and handed it back to Tula.

"As you can see, time is a means of currency and is necessary to live in this world, which is why I'm fascinated that you're here with what appears to be no time. Usually, when a writer first discovers their ability to enter this world, their transporter brings them here first. Their watches are presented to them with enough time to enter the time bank and refill the watch, but this wasn't the case for you."

I felt like a kid who was sent to school without money for lunch.

"Tula, this isn't the first place I've traveled to. I've been entering other cities for weeks now without knowing about the watch. It never presented itself to me before today. I only arrived here after finding Grandpa's journal about this place. I used the writing table to get here."

Tula bit her lip and released a sigh as she searched her mind for the most logical question to ask.

"How did you find the writing table?"

"It was Grandpa's. He kept it in a room in his house, and a few years after his disappearance, it was moved to my house. I sat at the table one day while reading a story I wrote, and suddenly I was in the story."

Tula looked like she was working out a puzzle. She looked at me, then at the floor. I could tell she knew something, but she was hesitant to reveal it.

"Tula, what is it? You know something. I can see it in your face."

She laid her hands flat on the table. "There is one possible explanation I'm familiar with, a legend, a story that's as old as time itself and may explain how you're here with no time on your watch," she said.

Our food arrived, and Tula took a huge bite of her omelet as I stared at her with anticipation, shocked that I even had to demand she finish what she was going to tell me.

"Well, are you going to tell me your supposed theory based on this legend you've heard of?"

"Sorry, yes, the legend." She placed her fork on the table and took a quick swig of her tea before continuing. "There's this story about how an old wooden table was constructed from this tree that possessed some kind of magical power. The table allowed the person who possessed it to travel to fictional worlds without being touched by time.

"Apparently, the man who planted the tree chopped off one of the branches, and within seconds a new branch grew where the old one was removed. The man took several branches and constructed a table, and upon its completion he discovered it took him to the places he wrote about. The table possessed a special power that protected the writer from harm so the stories could be brought back to his people. The table is supposedly under guard, though, and no one has reported it missing."

"Do you think I stole the writing table?"

"No, of course not. I'm just trying to think of how it's possible you're here with no time on your watch."

If I was there by the magic of Grandpa's writing table, I wondered if there were other ways writers traveled.

"Do all writers travel by a writing table?" I asked.

Tula glanced down at her plate of food and then sat back in her chair.

"No, they use various writing objects: pens, notebooks, magical ink. Stuff like that," she said.

But she revealed that no one understood how the objects got their powers. The only common thread was that the owners only recalled the objects being passed down from one family member to the next.

We ate our breakfast with haste in a race to beat the questions that began to fill our heads.

When the last bite had been consumed and not a drop of tea was left, Tula pushed our plates to the side and said, "Come on!" and jumped up and grabbed my arm. She practically dragged me from my seat and out of the diner. I pulled away from her as soon as we exited the building.

"Slow down! Where are we going?"

"We need to find out more about the writing table, and I have a book at home that might give us more information," she said.

I turned to look at the Timer Diner one last time and noticed the crown symbol on the building again.

"What is that symbol on the building?" I asked.

"That is Anschauung's Crown. Haven't you ever heard of it?" she responded as she continued to jog ahead of me.

"As a matter of fact, I haven't heard of it. What is it?" I asked, running behind her, the contents of my breakfast swishing around in my stomach.

"I'll explain everything back at my house."

I followed her around the corner to what looked like a phone booth—just without a phone. Tula pulled me in and closed the door.

At the back of the booth, there was a scroll mounted on the wall. She pulled down the scroll, which I noticed had several tick marks on it, and her fingers rolled down the list as it unfolded. She gave one of the tick marks a strong thump with her index finger.

In a matter of seconds, we were transported to the outside of a brick cottage with a neon blue door accented with several potted pink flowers. The walls of the cottage were overgrown with red- and green-leafed vines, and one hung in front of the door. Clumps of green moss emerged from the cracks and crevices of the cottage. The stone was broken in several places, revealing red brick and orange clay thrown on top of each other. The blue door was tall and featured a brass knob in the center. Just above the knob was a decorated brass peephole.

I followed Tula as she went up to the door, peeped through the hole, and then turned the knob.

"Why did you look through the peep hole?"

"How else would the house know I lived here?"

"You don't use a key?"

Tula pushed the door open for me, "Our homes are our personal spaces, so entry shall only be granted to its residents."

Inside Tula's home was the grandest library I'd ever seen.

From the outside the cottage looked small, like a two-bedroom home with a quaint living space and kitchen. But inside, there were twenty-foot-high ceilings and elaborate paintings that reminded me of the works of Michelangelo: angels in clouds, women dancing in fields, old men with long white beards. The walls were floor-to-ceiling bookcases bursting with leather-bound novels rustic in color and appeared aged by their tattered spines.

A wheeled ladder stood against one of the bookcases, and open books littered the wooden floor below. It was a fantastic sight to see so many books. I could see several rooms just like it that tunneled to the other side of the house, which looked a mile wide.

I stood in the middle of the arched hallway, feeling small.

"I know. I have a problem—collecting books is my passion," Tula said, a fingernail between her teeth.

"This is your house?"

"Yes, I know. It's not much, but it's home to me!"

Not much would have been the small wooden shelf above my bed with a few of my favorite books. Tula's house was a grand museum of writers, and her collection far exceeded any public library I had ever been to.

"Are you kidding? It's unbelievable! How long have you been collecting all of these books?"

"I don't know. I guess a hundred years or so."

"One hundred years? How's that possible?" I asked. She didn't look much older than forty.

"You see, I was born in the Time Table, so I age at a slower rate than those born outside the Time Table. We are given an allotment of five hundred years and will age faster as we get closer to the end of our allotment."

I tried to imagine for a moment what it would be like knowing I could possibly live for five hundred years. I recalled how people looked at one hundred—their frail, bony, wrinkly bodies barely holding on—and then I tried to visualize living that way for another one hundred years and then another and so on until I was close to five hundred. I would surely be nothing but dust.

"Five hundred years! That seems like an unbearably long time to live."

"I guess it would seem long to you, but our ancestors used to live for a thousand years. Maybe over time, it was too long and our given time allotment was shortened?"

It was simply not possible for me to fathom living one thousand years.

"I have to admit, being a timekeeper and living for hundreds of years does have its downsides," Tula said. "I see writers die all the time and their stories vanish. Writers I befriend and become close with die in a world I've never been to. I will say, thankfully, none of my writers have run out of time because I failed to remind them."

"Yeah, what exactly does a timekeeper do?"

Tula talked as I scanned her elaborate book collection. I took my time running my finger down each spine, examining the title and author. Most of her collection was hardcover books, but I noticed a few were paperback, their spines torn at the top and bottom from being read so many times.

"I act as a liaison, a broker, and a personal assistant to a small group of writers to remind them when the time allotment on their watch is due for a refill. A lot of writers keep a pretty close eye on when they need more time, but some forget, so I remind them."

I was so enthralled with my newfound ability to create such fascinating worlds, I couldn't imagine ever forgetting to fill my watch.

"A writer needs time from the bank so they can remain in their stories, and their time is also used to sustain the lives of the worlds they've created. If they run out of time, they're locked out from our world and their stories eventually disappear."

I pictured my mother reminding me of my weekly chores. Remembering to fill my watch with time so I didn't die and the worlds in which I created did not die seemed desperately out of place and almost comical.

"How do you send them reminders?"

"Well, if they visit me often, I'll look at their watch and tell them how much time is left, but if I haven't seen them in a while, I'm able to send them a message using a special tablet that carves messages on the back of their watches."

I remembered the curious message on the back of my watch and pulled it from my pocket.

"Did you write this message?" I said as I handed my watch to Tula. Tula examined the back of the watch.

Time is mastered in a series of four
with each taking dichotomy explored.
If you are wise the Guards will see
collecting them all will set us free.

"What a strange riddle," Tula said. "I don't recall writing this. I wonder who it was sent from."

I sighed and looked back at all the books. "Have you read all of these?"

"Most of them. Some I just picked up because I loved the binding or heard about the timeline."

I walked farther down the hallway and saw that each room had a couple of windows allowing just enough natural light to catch the gold-embossed lettering on some of the books on Tula's shelves. Each room also had various seating options, from chairs and sofas to daybeds.

I walked over to a book with a red binding and opened it. The paper was yellow, and the handwritten words were broken and faded. I placed the book back on the shelf.

"Tula, how did you meet Grandpa?"

She sat in a green chair and relaxed as she talked. "I came across his timeline at work one day. I actually found it on the floor outside of the Master Timekeeper's office. He's my boss. He ensures all timelines are recorded efficiently and accurately. He has access to all the timelines at the registrar's office. I was lucky to get a job working under him. I sometimes get to read stories of interest."

Tula explained that stories of interest were worlds or characters created to dismantle the Time Table. Some writers did not like the idea of someone keeping tabs on their stories and therefore created characters to overthrow the order of the Time Table.

As Tula continued to talk, I found out that Grandpa had written several stories of interest before he found out about his ability to travel to them. She assured me though that Grandpa's stories were found to be harmless. One was about a farmer who caught tornadoes for a living and kept them in a corral at his ranch. I kind of remembered that one from when I was a child. Tula found that story unique and worked closely with the Master Timekeeper to make sure she was notified when Grandpa first arrived at the Time Table.

They met in the courtyard, much the same way Tula had greeted me. From then on, Tula was Grandpa's timekeeper, and they built a lasting friendship—at least until the time change.

"Your grandfather was never a threat, and the man who captured tornadoes was completely benevolent. The last time I saw your grandfather was the day before the time change. He said he needed a refill on his watch. He said he was working on a magnificently complex story that would require a lot of time. That was just the kind of thing he would do, create elaborate worlds that required his constant attention. But he did a brilliant job of keeping up with them all."

Tula's words made me realize that creating a story of my own was not as simple as it seemed. Without my drive to keep the story alive, it would vanish and everyone who was a part of it would cease to exist.

"After the time change, the Master Timekeeper kept a close lock and key on timelines, and my attempts to find out what happened to your grandfather were unsuccessful. During the first year of the time change, I wondered if it was even possible to find out what happened to him, as we discovered some portions of the writers' timelines were destroyed and taken out of the register."

She took a book from a nearby shelf, removed a key from inside the pages, and then walked toward a glass case in the middle of the room. Inside the case was a collection of five books. She opened the case and removed one that was bound in what appeared to be hair and handed it to me.

"Here, this was a book your grandfather gave me the last time I saw him. He said he wrote it for me. The cover is horsehair."

I took the book in my hands and opened to the first page. The words were written in ink that burned like embers, similar to the writing on the back of my pocket watch. Within seconds, the text rose from the page and formed images in the air. I watched as a line of text took the form of a white horse that began to gallop on the page, and then more words formed into a landscape of an open field covered in red flowers and a sky that was hazy under a red and orange sun. The horse kicked at the words, and they scattered with every stomp of its hooves. The words melted together and changed colors. The horse's mane blew in the wind as it galloped.

I looked up at Tula, and she smiled with excitement.

"I've always wanted to see someone else's reaction to that!" she said.

"The words are coming to life!" I said.

"It's pretty phenomenal, right?" she responded.

She moved in closer and knelt in front of the book. We watched the horse continue to gallop across the page.

"Your grandfather was no ordinary writer. This was something I had never seen in any of my previous writers or any of my friends' writers. This was different. The story came to life right before my eyes. I did some research, and I think the images are able to come to life by using a special ink."

I turned the page of the book, and again, the words leapt off the page and transformed. The horse stood at the edge of a river lined with dogwood trees in full bloom. Beneath the trees, bundles of azaleas with bright red, pink, and purple flowers exploded with color. A wooden plank walkway started under one of the dogwoods and moved along the edge of the azaleas, extending over the river.

On the next page, a bridge formed and led to a cove where a large castle sat in the middle of a narrow piece of rock that rose high out of the water and into the clouds. At the base of the rock, a canoe floated in the water next to a ladder that extended to an arched doorway into the castle. I turned the page again and saw several canoes with canvas tops floating in a harbor against a red sunset.

Tula pulled another book from the glass case. This one was the largest and thickest among the five books inside the case. She opened to the table of contents and flipped to a page titled "The Guardians of Twelve."

"This is the book I think might help us find out more about your table."

I closed Grandpa's book and handed it back to Tula.

"What is it?" I asked.

"This is a history book about the Time Table. This chapter chronicles the Guardians of Twelve and the elusive writing table."

"What are the Guardians of Twelve?"

Just then there was a knock at Tula's door. Tula closed the book and placed it back in the case.

THE GUARDIANS OF TWELVE

Tula looked through the peephole, opened the door, and greeted a large man in a blue robe the color of Tula's door. A knotted gold rope around his waist gleamed whenever the light coming from outside hit it. His shoulder-length white hair curled at the ends. His round face was adorned with a handlebar mustache the same color as his hair.

He greeted Tula, and she gave him a friendly handshake and curtsy. She motioned for him to come into the seating area.

"Hello, young fellow. I'm Asia Scatterback. I'm the Master Time-keeper."

I was always nervous around important officials. My hands sweated, and I felt cautious and self-conscious.

"Pleased to meet you, sir," I said, and I held out my hand. "I'm Alden Rowe."

"Ah, yes, I've heard of you and your grandfather."

I smiled and looked back at Tula, unsure of what to say next.

"Mr. Scatterback, would you care for some refreshment?" Tula asked.

"No, thank you. I think we have some business to get down to."

"What brings you here today?" she said and motioned to Mr. Scatterback to have a seat in one of the green velvet chairs.

"One of my senior officials said you presented a watch today that would not accept time. Is that correct?" he asked sternly.

I felt like I'd been accused of doing something wrong, and my nerves became elevated, making my ears turn red and my voice shake.

"Uh...yes, that's true," I said and looked to Tula to give me some kind of advice.

"Mr. Scatterback, do you have any idea what prevented Alden's watch from accepting time?" Tula asked.

Mr. Scatterback ignored Tula and asked me to show him the watch. I pulled it from my pocket and handed it to him. He examined it just as the other clerks had, but stopped when he read the inscription on the back.

"Curious, this inscription. Do you know who wrote it?" he asked.

I shook my head.

He removed a vial from his pocket. It was filled with a purple substance mixed with something clear.

"I'm going to use a special solution that will reveal if there are any hidden secrets about this watch."

He held the watch in his palm and placed a few drops of liquid on it. The substance split into two halves: the purple part, which looked like it had the consistency of oil, spread across one side of the watch, and the clear part of the solution, which looked like water, spread across the other side. I waited for something to happen, but the two parts just dropped off the watch and into Mr. Scatterback's hand.

"How unusual—it seems to have deflected the solution," he said. "Alden, I think it's best I take this back to the registrar's office and do some more tests. Tula, will you bring him by tomorrow afternoon? I shall return the watch to you then."

Tula cleared her throat. "Sir, would it be better if Alden went with you while you perform the tests?"

Mr. Scatterback narrowed his eyes and said firmly, "I'm sure Alden has no objections with me taking the watch today and returning it to him tomorrow. Do you, boy?"

Mr. Scatterback made it clear this conversation was going to go his way, so I agreed to let him take the watch. Tula escorted him to the door, and we watched him make his way down the street.

"I think there's something about that watch that he doesn't want us to know," she said.

I agreed, and we sat back down in the library. What could he possibly think was wrong with my watch? I felt extremely uncomfortable that I allowed Mr. Scatterback to take my watch without question. It felt wrong to have been so yielding to his demands, and I wondered if I would ever see the watch again. Tula could see the panic in my eyes and tried to calm me.

"I wouldn't worry too much about it. The worst they will do is run some additional tests for whatever reason, and besides, if Tell Tale Solution doesn't reveal anything, then there is nothing to hide—and if it is hiding something and can withstand the effect of the solution from the Tell Tale Well, then nothing will crack its secret," Tula said.

"What was the solution called?"

"It's a mixture from the Tell Tale Well. A special blend of oil and water."

I looked at her as if she was a crazy lady running in circles while shouting gibberish, and her quick segue to offering me some tea made me believe she could not bear to see me looking at her that way.

"I'll put the kettle on, and we will have a cup of tea. I believe I have some biscuits left in the tin."

Tula took the history book back out of the glass case and handed it to me. She then turned and made her way toward the kitchen. I followed her with the history book about the Time Table, flipping through the pages along the way and bookmarking with my finger the chapter on the Guardians of Twelve.

As we approached the kitchen, the room narrowed, pushing the floor and ceiling closer together. Tula pressed through an arched wooden door revealing a quaint kitchen much smaller than the grandness of her library.

To the left was a stone, wood-burning fireplace that was flush with the floor and flanked by a large diamond-shaped window on each side. On the right was a U-shaped kitchen overlooking a bay window with a long wooden table in front and equally long church pews on both sides for sitting.

"Make yourself comfortable while I gather us some refreshments," Tula said.

I sat at the table and saw a lush garden outside the window. Tulips grouped in every color lined the outer perimeter, and the garden was full of buzzing bees and dancing butterflies.

"Pretty, isn't it?" Tula asked while she lit the stove.

"Yes, quite mesmerizing."

"Some people find gardening to be too much work, but a vision like that is worth it I say."

I turned my attention back to the book about the Guardians of Twelve and skimmed over the first page.

"So, tell me what the Guardians of Twelve are," I said.

"The Guardians of Twelve are people who've sworn to protect twelve unique objects that, when combined, are said to bring items from our world into your world. Taking what is fictional and making it a reality."

"That sounds awesome."

"No, the Guardians are in place to prevent that from happening. You see, bringing something from a story into the writer's world can be dangerous. Allowing an imaginary object into a writer's world could have tremendous and chaotic repercussions and cause a disruption in the natural order of your world."

I thought of a dragon being brought into my home.

"I guess you're right."

"Should a single person possess all twelve objects, they would have the power to bring our world to its knees. They would have the power to control the Time Table and all the stories registered with the Grandfather Clock. Rumors are already circulating that's the reason for the time shift. Some people believe someone has stolen all of the items, causing the time disruption."

The Guardians of Twelve sounded like an army of fortitude that would be impenetrable should someone have tried to steal their precious objects, but Tula explained there were twelve separate groups of guardians for each object throughout the land.

"Do you believe someone has really defied the Guardians and stolen all of the objects?"

"Mr. Scatterback confirmed with the Guardians that all of the objects are still under protection, so I don't know what else to believe."

"What are these twelve objects, anyway?"

"The twelve objects balance all the imaginary worlds written in books and possess special powers. Each object represents the literary elements used to create a story," Tula said.

She then sat beside me and pointed at the list on the page and read aloud each description.

"The Writer – Before a story can begin, an idea must be born from the writer. Without the writer, all of the other objects serve no purpose because if the idea of a world does not exist, then we do not exist."

This made perfect sense to me, but how it translated into a guarded object was still not clear to me.

"Is someone guarding one superior writer somewhere?" I asked.

"No, but each writer has their own guard, someone who looks after their best interests."

I still didn't understand, and my vacant expression made Tula continue.

"Someone who ensures they never run out of time."

Then it clicked. Tula wasn't just my timekeeper but also my guardian.

"Think about what would happen if all the worlds and their inhabitants you created died because you forgot to load your pocket watch."

I smiled and nodded in agreement with Tula. She smiled back and continued.

"The second object is the Tell Tale Well and represents character – A bottomless well containing oil and water used to separate truth from lies, and shows us if one's character is built upon truth or lies. This is what Mr. Scatterback used on your watch. A few drops of it on your writing table should tell us if it's the legendary one. Some of the solution is imported into the Time Table for the very purpose of protecting our worlds from portentous plots."

I wondered if I could use the solution from the Tell Tale Well to reveal where Grandpa was located, and what other powers from the list of objects might help me find him faster. I looked back to the list, signaling Tula to continue.

"The Story Book, which represents plot – A book with the most influential stories in history. Stories that have influenced the masses and created a pivotal change in history.

"The fourth object is the Lantern of Ayla, which represents theme – It contains a light bright enough to permeate the darkest of hearts and is fueled by a countless number of happy thoughts and memories. It was created to show us the most powerful theme of any story—love."

I hadn't told Tula that Babacan had given me the Lantern of Ayla or that I had already once used it in the forest. I wasn't quite sure I was ready to disclose that piece of information yet, especially considering the object was supposed to be guarded at that very moment.

"The next object is Polyglot's Tongue, representing language. This is a casing in the shape of a tongue. When someone inserts their own tongue inside the casing, they have the ability to speak any language in any world."

I rolled my tongue inside my mouth and tried to imagine how I would ever be able to talk with something over it.

"The sixth object is the Narrator's Voice, which obviously stands for voice. This is a tiny megaphone that has the ability to produce gigantic sound waves. It's said to have the ability to flatten mountains.

"The seventh object is just as powerful—Anschauung's Crown, a crown of silver and trimmed with blue sapphires that can read the mind of anyone around. This powerful insight represents narrative mode or point of view, allowing the wearer to see a different perspective, the same way you would write a story from someone else's view."

"This was the crown on the outside of the Timer Diner, right?"

"Correct, the buildings in the Time Table each represent a number that stands for the number of guards for each object. Anschauung's Crown has seven guards."

It occurred to me then that each building was in the shape of the number it represented. The Timer Diner wasn't a triangle. It was in the shape of the number seven, and the time bank was in the shape of the number twelve.

"The courtyard is one giant clock," I said.

"Correct."

Tula continued, "The Setting Ink represents setting, and with a single drop can create breathtaking landscapes.

"The ninth object is the Mood Ring, which represents mood and tone. The person who wears the ring can change the attitudes of anyone in their presence. If you wanted to make people happy, you could just think of something happy while wearing the ring and anyone around you would feel the same way. If you wanted someone to feel sad, all you have to do is think of something sad."

Her finger glided down to the tenth object.

"The next three are the most powerful and heavily guarded. The Dueling Stones stand for conflict in the way that a story will have two opposing forces. Clicking the two stones together generate a large ball of fire and, as you can imagine, can be quite dangerous.

"The eleventh object is the Writer's Table, which represents structure. A magical table that allows whoever possesses it to roam freely through time without ever aging, and of course it is the foundation on which the other elements are constructed."

"Is this the same table you think I possess? My table is made of wood, and if Mr. Scatterback confirmed all of the objects were still under guard—and *heavily under guard*, as you put it—then it seems even more unlikely that I would be in possession of *the* Writer's Table."

"Well, maybe not, but it is mysterious that you appear to be traveling without any time, which is so famously an attribute of the Writer's Table," Tula said.

The writing table was heavy, but it was because it was made of oak, not stone. I knew little about both tables, so I saw no point is further arguing with Tula.

"What's the final object?" I asked.

"The Pendulum of Time, which is all encompassing of the life of a writer and their story and is part of the Grandfather Clock at the time bank."

The twelve objects were no doubt powerful and also dangerous. Tula closed the book and looked me straight in the eyes to ensure I listened to her next words.

"The guards must protect the objects. As I said before, anyone who got their hands on all of them would be a force to reckon with. They could change any story they wished. They could wipe out worlds and populations in the blink of an eye. Every story you've grown to love could change drastically or be erased altogether. Our stories could be abolished from everyone's memories."

I pondered the idea of reading a book and having it expunged from my memory. I could read *The Swiss Family Robinson* on Monday and by Tuesday I would never know I'd ever read it or that it even existed. Everyone would be at the mercy of the one holding all the power. I thought carefully about Tula's words. She was jumping to the conclusion that only something terrible would happen. Was it possible to do something great with it?

"You're assuming that anyone who has the power would cause destruction?" I asked Tula.

Her expression went flat, and her eyes seemed to darken with fear.

"Well, it's happened before, and I can imagine the greed that would eventually come with having so much power," she said.

"It's happened before?"

Tula explained that thousands of years ago when the objects were created, they sat quietly scattered across many lands, unguarded and untouched by any literary character.

Eventually, they were discovered, and the magic each one possessed helped protect the world it resided in from being forgotten. When stories are forgotten, the worlds that made up the story crumble and all the inhabitants die, but these objects helped preserve many of the stories for centuries.

It wasn't long before a man with a skeleton-like face and a bone-chilling laugh plotted to take the objects by force, and when he found himself in possession of them all, he unleashed an evil like no one had ever seen.

I felt my own eyes deepen with fear as I recalled my encounter with a similar skeleton-like character.

"The skeleton had a name. They called him the Macabre. His appearance often transformed into horrific forms depending on an individual's darkest fears," Tula said.

"Like spiders and bats?" I asked.

Tula shook her head.

"You would be surprised how many people think that, but the manifestation of just a spider or a bat is not what really scares people."

I took a hard swallow.

"It's the fear of what a spider or a bat can do given no boundaries."

I thought about it but quickly pushed the thought from my head. I didn't want any recollection of it in my mind. If I pushed the thought away quickly, perhaps I would forget about it altogether.

Tula could sense I did not want to dwell on her words, so she continued with her story.

"The Macabre gathered all of the objects at the Writer's Table and began to unleash his evil all around him.

"Characters turned to dust and blew away in the wind, and dark clouds filled with poison were cast over surrounding towns, killing everyone and replacing their cities with nothing but ash and fire. With the extent of his destruction reaching as far as he imagined, he created an object of his own, a fleshy black mass that fit in his hand and wiggled with repugnance.

"He captured a traveling writer and attached the mass to his body, where it seeped beneath the writer's skin and quickly took over his insides. The writer begged the Macabre to remove it, but he was unwilling and watched over the writer as he died from the mass.

"The Macabre created more of these infectious masses and sent them back to your world with other writers, and slowly they died, taking all their stories and characters with them. It was a tragic discovery that the one who possessed all of the objects could create something and send it back into the worlds of our writers.

"The Guardians were chosen from each village from which the objects were stolen to fight the Macabre, but none could overthrow such evil, until when all hope was lost, a little girl appeared out of nowhere and confronted the evil skeleton. With his hand held toward the sky, the Macabre conjured a tremendous ball of darkness that rose high in the air. The darkness was created to smite the child from existence, but she was not afraid. Those watching in the distance saw this brilliant display of defiance and ran to save her.

"As the ball of darkness descended upon her, she stood on the Writer's Table with the other objects at her feet and held her hand out, commanding the ball to stop. The ball moved swiftly toward her, and when the mass hit her hand, an immense explosion radiated outward from the Writer's Table. When the explosion subsided, the Macabre and the little girl were gone, and only the objects remained. The Guardians each took an object and swore to protect them from such evil ever happening again."

The steam from the teakettle began pouring out, and Tula rounded the table to fill our cups. While the tea diffused, she placed a plate of cookies on the table.

"Have some," she said. "I made them last night, and they are a delight, plus they will take us out of this terrible story we've just discussed."

I took a bite of the cookie. It tasted like a mix of chocolate and spice with a slight hint of mint.

"I'll put the book back. After that inquiry, Mr. Scatterback may return with more questions and I don't want to give him any ideas about our assumptions," she said as she closed the book containing the chapter on the Guardians of Twelve.

As the image of the Macabre subsided, a voice inside my mind came to the forefront. It was Babacan pleading for me to save them.

"Tula, although I would love to know if the writing table is the magical one, I still need to find Grandpa. If I can find him, maybe he can fix the time shift. You can track a writer at the registrar's office, right?"

Tula nodded in agreement.

"Do you think we can find Grandpa and see where he was last recorded?" I asked.

"The timeline should reveal the place your grandfather last visited, but Mr. Scatterback won't let anyone in the room where we keep the time logs without a justified cause."

"Can't we just tell him if we find Grandpa, we could solve the time shift problems?"

Tula sighed. "Something tells me that would not be in our best interest."

I followed Tula back into the library and watched her place the history book we had been reading back inside the glass case.

After the book was tucked among the others in the case, she turned to me and said, "I have my suspicions, but for now I will keep them to myself. Don't worry, though. I will explain in due course, but for now we will need to think of a way to sneak into the registrar's office."

She smiled the kind of smile that promised risk and adventure. She took my hand, and we darted out of the cottage.

THE REGISTRAR'S OFFICE

We ran on a cobblestone walkway to another booth down the street. With one swoop, Tula held my hand and tapped the scroll with her finger—and we were back at the courtyard.

We planned to enter the registrar's office after everyone had left for the day. Despite the time constantly changing, some of the clocks were not affected by the shift, which allowed a few people to keep track of what time it actually was. Tula explained most of the older antique clocks around the city were uninterrupted and kept on ticking as if nothing had happened. A few of those clocks were brought into local businesses such as the time bank and the registrar's office, which helped in establishing when people could leave for the day.

I walked ahead of her and motioned for her to follow me into the alley where the writing table remained.

"I wanted to make sure it was still here. I wasn't sure if Mr. Scatterback saw me arrive with it. Plus, we have a pretty good view of the time bank from here, and we can think of a way to get in the building undetected," I said.

The courtyard was empty, but we could see that the security guards had started their rounds. They circled the building and checked the side doors.

"We'll get in, find the register, and get out before anyone notices. It should be easy, since I know the layout," Tula said.

"That easy, huh?" I asked skeptically.

"The registrar's office is under constant surveillance."

Tula explained that two guards patrolled the lobby and the buildings outside perimeter and a third guard sat in the control room watching the monitors that were connected to cameras through the building and surrounding courtyards.

She suggested we enter the building using an exterior door to the left of the front entrance. The peephole in the door would recognize her and allow us access. The left door was hidden by a wide evergreen tree and rarely used unless in the event of a mass evacuation of the building. The door had a single security camera that often was obscured by the tree branches when the evergreen went too long in between pruning.

"How do you know so much about the security of the building?" I asked.

"Uh…let's just say I have my connections."

Although it sounded like a good plan for gaining access to the building, it was unclear to us if the camera was indeed obscured by the overgrown tree. We wouldn't know until we were standing at the door, and by then the guard in the control room would have already detected us.

"Any ideas on how to get past the guards?" I asked.

"I'm thinking," Tula responded.

I clenched my fists inside my pockets and tried to think of a distraction for the guards. My right hand hit something in my pocket, and I pulled it out. It was the Lantern of Ayla, in its blue cloth bag.

If I whispered, "Ayla," the lantern would explode into a ball of light and be the perfect distraction. Tula and I could then sneak in through the side entrance.

"We're going to use this as the distraction," I said, the bag in my palm.

Tula's eyebrows rose. "What is in the bag?"

I reached in and removed the lantern. I assumed Tula, who earlier told me all about the twelve objects, would instantly recognize the lantern as *the* Lantern of Ayla, but she had no clue what I was holding when I presented it to her.

"It's the Lantern of Ayla," I explained.

"But...how...?"

"I'll explain later. Just follow me, and I'll show you what it can do. When the next round of darkness arrives, follow my lead," I said.

Tula nodded, and as soon as it grew dark, we bolted toward one of the nearby buildings. Daylight quickly approached, so we waited until it was dark again before making our way to the next building. I held the lantern in my palm, whispered, "Ayla," and threw it in the air. The lantern exploded with a million colors.

Multiple rays of turquoise, copper, and chartreuse beamed toward the building. The spectrum of colors shot directly through the front doors and hit the glass façade of the lobby, bending the wavelength of colors in all directions.

Within minutes, all three guards were alerted and ran out to see the spectacle.

Tula and I dashed for the side door as beams of amber and crimson bounced off the front glass doors, captivating the guards.

When we made it to the side door undetected by the guards, we noticed the evergreen had uprooted itself and knocked the security camera off the building.

"The tree must have been knocked backwards when the lantern exploded," Tula said.

She positioned her eye in front of the peephole, and the door unlocked for us. Tula pulled the door open, and we entered a dimly lit hallway. Tula pointed to a stairway up ahead.

"Those steps will lead us to the west wing of the building, where the registrar's office is," she said.

In our ascent up the stairs, I tried to listen for any sign of the guards following us. Our rapid breathing from the run and the swift movement of our feet created more noise than I wanted. At the top of the steps, Tula pulled open a heavy metal door.

Her eyes were focused straight ahead, but I was entranced by the magnitude of the room we entered. The floors were shiny white marble and reflected a blue glow from the adjacent walls. Beams of electric blue climbed the walls of the thick, textured columns that stood strong like soldiers protecting a citadel. Weaved among the columns were a set of winding staircases that led to a second-level promenade. Tula pulled me along.

We climbed one of the staircases and arrived at the second-floor promenade, where I was equally in awe of the beauty of the room. On the second floor were rows of long crystal boxes the size of sofas. Above each one hung a pendant that emitted a beautiful string of white light. Tula rushed toward one, and I followed.

I watched her complete a combination of taps on the side of the crystal box, and then the front opened like a cabinet drawer. I leaned over to look inside and saw thousands of tubular crystals, each marked with a letter.

"Just tap the tops, and it will tell you the name on the register," Tula said as she tapped one and a name projected in the air above the tube.

I noticed most of the tubes we were looking through had the letter *R* embossed on top of them.

"Does it go by last name or first?" I asked.

"Last name."

I started tapping a few and watched as the names popped up: Rand, Raskin, and Rawls.

"Shouldn't we be looking through the *C*s? Grandpa's pen name is Cal Caulder."

"No, the register recognizes the writer's birth name."

I continued tapping the crystals and watched as more names popped up: Reynolds, Richards, and Riggs. When I tapped on Riggs, unlike the others, a string of wispy light appeared and was attached to the pendant above the drawer.

"Whoa! What is that?" I asked Tula.

Tula had practically buried her head in the ocean of tubular crystals, and after a brief moment, she finally looked up at me.

"Be careful!"

Her tone of alarm scared me, and I pulled my hand back, hitting it on the side of the drawer.

"What does that string of light mean?" I asked.

"That light means the author is currently writing a story. The light attached to it feeds to the pendant above, which then registers the time-line."

Tula gently tapped the top of the crystal for Riggs, and the light disappeared.

"If you come across any more of those, just be extra careful when tapping the top. Now, let's hurry. I'm not sure how long we can hold off those guards."

I continued tapping more crystals: Riordan, Roach, and Rowling.

When we reached the *Ss*, we realized Grandpa's name was not in the drawer.

"No luck?" I asked.

Tula paused. "Wait. We usually put files of interest in another room, but we will need something extra to help us enter that room. Follow me," she said.

We retraced our steps back down the winding staircase, and Tula approached a sitting area off to the right. She frantically opened a few drawers revealing a mess of papers crammed in the back of each one. I stood on the other side and examined a stack of books lined neatly on top of the desk. The spine of one of the books said *Rowe*.

"Is this Grandpa's?" I asked.

Tula dug her hands and arms deeper into the back of a drawer.

"Yes. Those are a collection of your Grandpa's books—I got it!" she exclaimed.

She pulled her arm out of the drawer and revealed a dusty vial of purple liquid—Tell Tale Solution.

"I knew I had some," she said.

"This is *your* desk?"

"Yes, this is where I sit and do all that is needed from the secretary to the Master Timekeeper," she said sarcastically.

Without further discussion, we quickly ran back up the winding staircase and followed a curved hallway that ended in front of a floor-to-ceiling tiled image of a stone wishing well complete with a shingled roof and attached bucket. A set of three small steps led to a ledge in front of the picture.

"I've always wanted to do this. I've been in here before, but I've never been given the opportunity to open the door myself," Tula said.

She poured some of the Tell Tale Solution on the ledge, and we watched as the liquid split in half; the purple oil traveled up along the left side of the picture, and the clear part of the solution moved along the edge of the right side. When the two sides met in the middle, the picture faded away and revealed the entryway into a disorderly room full of odd objects and trinkets.

Unlike the neat and organized first and second floors of the registrar's office, this room looked more like a cluttered attic jam-packed with an eclectic bunch of novelties. I saw gold cups, feathered spheres, and a coat rack with snakeheads as hooks. We shuffled in between enormous wooden armoires with carvings of different mythical creatures such as a griffin, a mermaid, and a centaur. I had to be careful not to knock over several oversized chairs stacked to the ceiling, and mountains of broken reading glasses and torn books.

I followed Tula to the back of the room where we found several more filing cabinets, only these were not the crystal kind we previously rummaged through. The cabinets in the back of the room were taller and made of black granite. They did not have a lighted pendant above them, and their isolated location and darkness made me believe there would be no further stories written for these registers.

"Help me look in here," she said and opened one of the cabinets.

I pressed my chest against the cold drawer and tapped through the crystals, looking for Grandpa's register. Unlike the previous drawers, this cabinet was not alphabetized, and many of the crystals lay horizontal; some were even broken. There were so many registers of interest, all of them tossed among the drawer like garbage. I came across the names Bir, Hampton, Flynn, and Talibah. I remembered Babacan's last name was Talibah, but the first name listed was Massoud.

"I found it!" Tula exclaimed. She handed me Grandpa's register. Before I could ask any questions, we heard a fury of motion outside the door. We dropped to the floor and, in the process, knocked over a box that was sitting on top of the filing cabinet. The side of the box read, "TIME SHORTAGES."

Tula grabbed a handful of papers that fell out of the box and briefly read a description of someone who received an allotment of time. The paper argued that time rapidly diminished without the consent of the writer. The box was full of recorded mishaps with time allotment.

"This is news to me. I haven't heard of this before," Tula said. She grabbed another handful of disputes and quickly rolled them into her pocket. Then something underneath the papers caught her attention.

"I believe this is yours," she said, and handed me my pocket watch. "I wonder if Scatterback found anything intriguing about it."

"I wonder if he knows what the inscription means?" I asked.

I quickly stuffed the watch into my pocket, and we hid behind one of the armoires and watched two security guards enter the room. As they made their way down the center walkway, we crawled on our knees along the edge of the room toward the door.

Tula pulled the Tell Tale Solution from her pocket, then reached up to a nearby shelf and grabbed a flat slate with several black crows drawn across the top. She poured the solution onto the slate and slid it into the middle walkway. Suddenly the crows came to life and attacked the guards, giving us the chance we needed to scurry out undetected.

A commotion of fury erupted in the room as the guards swatted at the crows. We kept running until we reached the end of the hallway to catch our breath.

"Where do you think the third guard is?" I asked.

"I'm not sure, but let's not stick around to find out."

We dashed down the winding staircase and through the metal door, back down the side stairwell, and out the building's side entrance. Tula glanced around for any sign of the missing guard, but all was clear.

The Lantern of Ayla flashed and returned to my hand as we ran across the courtyard. We didn't stop until we reached the writing table. Looking back down the alley, we were relieved to see we hadn't been followed.

Crouched behind the writing table, I whispered, "How did you make those birds come to life?"

"Remember, the solution from the Tell Tale Well shows us one's true character. It works the same way on objects. By adding a bit of the solution on the slate, it revealed the hidden qualities and brought the crows to life, much the same way it revealed the picture leading to the room of interest was really an entrance to the room."

"But how did you know the crows would come to life like that?"

"It came across my desk a few weeks ago, and I remembered Mr. Scatterback telling me it contained special powers. That it held the birds captive, like a cage of sorts. I knew a few drops of solution would release them, and it did." She showed me the bottle. "But in a panic I used it all. I was going to use the remainder of it on your writing table."

We'd have to wait to see if the writing table was the legendary one.

She stuffed the vial into one of her pockets and pulled out the roll of papers she'd found in the time shortages box.

"What do they say?" I asked.

She unrolled a few to read some of the details. All the reports dated back two years or more and chronicled cases where writers filled their watches but returned hours later and stated the time had rapidly diminished without use. A writer with the last name Serreno said her watch was filled at 10:30 a.m. for 730 hours, but before she had even left the Time Table, it had only twenty minutes left.

"I wonder if this has something to do with why your watch wouldn't accept time," Tula said.

I looked down at the crystal tube in my hand.

"Well, I'm just glad we at least got Grandpa's register. Now how do you read it?"

Tula took the crystal, and with her index finger and thumb, she pressed down on both ends of the tube and then released. The tube grew longer, and a glass rectangle extended outward from the center. She gave the surface a few taps, and lines of information glittered on it.

"That's odd. Your grandfather's last location is gone. It's missing."

She turned the slab toward me. Sure enough, the last marking looked like it had been burned off the timeline. The last visible markings referenced a place called the Pelted Plains and, before that, Ayla City.

"Tula, I have to go to the Pelted Plains. I have to go there and see if anyone knows Grandpa. Maybe someone there can tell me where he went next."

I wondered if I would be able to find the Pelted Plains in Grandpa's journals.

Tula turned the slab around and tapped "THE PELTED PLAINS." A story appeared in Grandpa's handwriting, which I recognized from his book about the Time Table. I was able to scroll through the text on the tablet using my finger much like an e-reader.

"Now you can go there. Just read this at the writing table," Tula said.

Tula urgently pushed the register into my hands and said, "Go! Now! Before we're discovered!"

There were still questions to be answered, though: Why did my watch not accept the time refill? What did the Master Timekeeper know? And why was time vanishing? Why was Grandpa's register in the interest room?

I tried to speak, but Tula told me to hurry.

I sat at the writing table and read about the Pelted Plains.

THE WIND WRANGLER

I arrived in a large field of green grass. The wind whipped at my pants, and my hair lashed my face as it thrashed around my head. Ominous dark clouds sat concentrated above me, spanning the entirety of the horizon. Hot and cold air rolled over the plains, like the air was plowing a path for an invisible monster.

An uneasy feeling of vulnerability took over, and I weighed the pros and cons of leaving the writing table. If I ventured too far and encountered something terrible, I might not be able to make it back to the writing table to escape. But I couldn't give up so quickly.

I pushed away from the table, walked forward, and looked above to make sure a tornado wasn't swirling. It sure looked like twister weather. Nothing scared me more than a tornado, a giant mass of wind and earth with no rules or boundaries and only one objective: to destroy anything in its path. I pictured my body tossed about in an unyielding vortex.

THE WIND WRANGLER

As I crossed the prairie, the clouds moved more rapidly. Within a few seconds, a funnel cloud formed. Terror rushed through me, and I turned and ran back toward the writing table. The wind blew strong at my back, and the tornado advanced in my direction. The smell of dirt and grass intensified, and the wind almost lifted me off the ground.

The tornado's quick release of wind blew me closer to the writing table. Each time I was knocked down, I quickly jumped to my feet and desperately reached for the writing table. With every fall, the tornado sucked the air back and pulled me with it. I felt like the tornado was tripping me on purpose in an effort to bring me closer to its perilous center.

I managed to get up each time and gain just enough ground to make me feel like I was getting closer, but the tornado never let up. Suddenly the tornado broke away from its pattern, and I ran as fast as I could toward the writing table. In the distance I saw a man on horseback galloping toward me. At the very moment I saw the man, I could feel the tornado pick up speed, expanding its swirling base. It was as if the sight of the man angered the tornado and it wanted to get to me before the man did. I was pitted between a large man on horseback and a violent tornado. I knew I would be sucked into the tornado if I stopped, so although I had no idea what the man would be like, at least he was human. The fear of being sandwiched between the two raced across my mind, but why was this man riding toward the tornado?

The wind closed in on me, and I felt my efforts to get away were useless. I was still too far from the writing table to escape. I looked at the man and screamed for help. The man and his horse stopped at the end of one of my screams. The man looked up at the twister from beneath his cowboy hat and held out his arm. A long black rope that started from his shoulder and wrapped around his arm to the middle of his palm sprang to life and leapt off his arm. The man took one end and began twirling the rope. The rope spun in rapid succession above his head, and then it shot in my direction. I dove for the ground, and the rope barely missed hitting my head.

When I looked up, I saw him holding the rope and the tornado twisting to get out of the other end.

A slight tug on the rope pulled the tornado toward me. I jumped up and ran toward the man in fear the tornado would run over me.

"You okay?" he shouted.

The man was much larger up close. He was very muscular, like someone I imagined as a bouncer at a concert, or someone who was security for the most popular celebrities. He wore a large white Stetson and rode a tan horse, eerily similar in color to his skin.

"Yes," I said in a ragged voice, tired from running from the twister.

The cowboy yanked the tornado, swung it to the right, and released the rope. The tornado followed his lasso's lead, and we watched it move precipitately off into the distance.

"Sorry about that," he said. "That one almost got away from me. It felt weak, though, so it should dissipate shortly."

The lasso that just released the tornado latched itself back on his arm and went back to its original form: a tattoo. I looked at him in confusion.

"I'm Dexas, local wind wrangler." He held his hand out. His hands, in thick brown suede gloves, swallowed my fingers.

114

"Hello, I'm Alden."

"Good to meet you. This here is my horse, Tallas. He helps me round up the tornadoes and get 'em to pasture. Well, if they're worth keepin'." He pet Tallas's mane.

"How did you do that with the tornado?" I asked.

"I'm a wind wrangler. I track tornadoes, harvest them, and keep them fenced in pastures back at the ranch," he said.

It was Dexas's mention of a ranch of tornadoes that made me remember the story Grandpa once told me. Dexas was the farmer who caught tornadoes.

"Come with me and I'll show you," he said.

He jumped on Tallas and offered me a hand. I obliged, and we took off. I tried to recall the details of the story Grandpa told me about Dexas, but the only thing I could remember was that he caught tornadoes.

A short ride later, we arrived at a ranch in the middle of a vast field. There was nothing in sight for miles, and since he claimed to be harvesting tornadoes, I understood why he had no neighbors. In the back of the field, there were ten or twenty spinning twisters.

"Those are tornadoes?" I asked in disbelief.

"Yes, of course. Haven't you been to a tornado ranch before?"

"No, I'm afraid not."

"Well, come on, let's get a closer look! Shall we?" he asked.

"Is it safe?"

He smiled, and we rode Tallas to the edge of the fence. The twisters were enormous close up. There were a variety of shapes, colors, and sizes. I watched a white one that looked similar to the one that almost consumed me. It was tall and skinny, swirled rapidly, and only moved slightly from side to side.

Another was a tremendously large classic wedge. One masked in a rain cloud looked almost greenish-yellow. But in the very back roared a particularly vicious and dangerous-looking large black tornado.

"That's Stoker. He's pretty sinister. I have to watch him because he sometimes consumes the other twisters. I'm working on a separate pen for him." He pointed to a half-circle of white steel in the far-left corner of the ranch.

"They have names? And what do you mean by 'consumes'?"

"Of course they have names. I don't raise them to slaughter and dissipate. That white one is Shivey." He pointed to the white tornado. "And that one is Stout, for obvious reasons." He pointed to the wedge-shaped twister.

I pointed to one I had almost missed. It was nearly translucent, like it hadn't quite formed.

"That one is Dusty. He's just an ol' dust devil. Not as strong as the others, but he's handy in helping me round 'em up," he said.

These tornadoes had names like common milk cows or livestock.

"What do you use the tornadoes for?" I asked.

"Well, mostly I use them to supply energy to the surrounding towns. Power's scarce since the time change, and since I had experience in wind wranglin', I thought I could make a few bucks while helpin' our townsfolk."

"What do you use to catch the tornadoes? I saw you had some kind of rope that wraps around them."

He held out his arm, and I watched the tattoo of the rope lift off his arm.

"Yep, it's a special rope. I was born with it. A gift, if you will. Only a select few are born with such a thing. Growin' up, people thought it was a defect, a curse from the man who once burnt these fields, but now folks are downright thankful people like me can stop tornadoes from destroyin' their towns."

"Does it hurt?"

"Sometimes, if I get a really big tornado, the rope feels like it's goin' to pull my insides out and I have to let it go. I wish I had one or two really thick, strong ones."

It was not easy for me to imagine someone hauling in a tornado, which I remembered reading could reach wind speeds over three hundred miles per hour.

"Your rope looks like the one wrapped around my grandpa's notebook."

I quickly removed the notebook from my pocket and held it out to Dexas.

He leaned in closer and pulled a glove off to run his hand across the rope that sealed the notebook.

"Well, I'll be. You're Colvin's grandson, aren't you?"

I smiled and nodded.

"I made the rope round that book you got there. I gave it to your grandfather a few years back. That man had a natural gift for catchin' tornadoes. It felt only right he should have a rope of his own."

I pictured Grandpa galloping across the plains, chasing tornadoes, racing the wind, and living an exciting life much different from the life I imagined he had grading papers and drinking tea at his desk.

"Do you know how to get the rope off the notebook?" I asked.

Dexas took the notebook in his hand.

"Where's the end of the rope?" he asked.

"I don't know. I even tried cutting it, but nothing has worked," I said.

Dexas smiled. "You wouldn't be able to cut this rope. If you could, it wouldn't be much use catching twisters, would it?"

"What's the rope made of?"

"Well, the rope is made of fibers that have been compounded by two unique stones. The rope is thin but holds together like reinforced steel. Pretty indestructible stuff. Easy to lasso round a tornado."

The wind picked up and forced me to look up at the clouds.

"Perfect tornado weather," Dexas said. "You want to see if we can catch us one?"

He must have been able to see the fear on my face.

"Don't worry! I do this all the time! It's completely safe! I won't put you in any real danger."

He *had* caught all of the other tornadoes. And it would be a good opportunity to ask him more questions about Grandpa, so I agreed.

"All right, let's do this!" he said, then howled into the sky.

I wondered if his joy was because, for a brief moment, he had remembered the good times he used to have with Grandpa. Or maybe the isolation of the prairie just gave him a hunger to meet new people.

THE WIND WRANGLER

Either way, I followed him to the barn, where I expected we would put on some protective gear and load into a tank-like vehicle.

Dexas threw a leather jacket into my lap.

"Put that on. Sometimes the air gets pretty cold."

I put the jacket on. It was made for a man two sizes larger than Dexas, but I figured the more padding I had, the better.

"Ever ridden a horse before?" he asked.

"No. Do I have to ride a horse on my own?"

"Nah, you can just ride on the back of mine," he said.

We hopped onto Tallas and headed into the open field. I looked over my shoulder, and the tornadoes in the pen got smaller and smaller as we galloped away.

We rode quickly and stopped on a hillside. Dexas searched the clouds for signs of tornadoes. I searched along with him.

The clouds moved speedily overhead. They swelled and rolled like a restless ocean, ready to crest with rain.

I felt insignificant up on that hillside, like a tiny ant looking out onto a field that never ended.

Dexas made a noise and pulled Tallas's reins, and we darted down the hillside and onto the open plain. Dexas's leather jacket blew into my face and blocked my view. I couldn't see, and I felt like I was going to be bucked off and left to wrangle a tornado on my own.

"We're close!" Dexas yelled over a burst of sudden wind. "Keep your eyes peeled!"

Suddenly, near the hillside we'd just left, dirt sprayed and wisps of spinning wind circulated above the crest.

"There!" I said, pointing to the hillside.

Dexas tugged Tallas, and we shot back toward the hill. The ferocious wind almost blew me right off Tallas's back, but the horse seemed unfazed and kept rumbling forward.

As we got closer, the tornado intensified like it was gearing up for a battle. But the closer we got, the more determined we became too. This tornado was ours. Inside I thought this, but I still had no idea what part I would play in capturing the tornado.

We suddenly came to a halt, and Dexas jumped off Tallas. Once he leapt from the horse, I saw the tornado, a midsize stovetop, in all its glory.

The massive twister teetered back and forth, sized us up, and waited to see who would make the first move.

Dexas extended his arm, and the tattoo once again came to life. As he moved closer to the tornado, he began to spin the lasso over his head. In one quick movement, like a bullet from a gun, he shot the lasso toward the tornado.

I gripped Tallas as tight as I could, fearing the tornado's impending charge.

The lasso crackled as it latched itself around the tornado's midsection. Dexas dug his boots in the ground and pulled tight. It was amazing to see man halt Mother Nature, something that could only be done within the confines of this world, a world created by Grandpa.

Dexas steadied himself, pulled the tornado back toward us, and handed me the rope. "Hold this while I get back on."

The rope vibrated tremendously, and my hands turned purple because I gripped it so tightly.

120

"You think you can manage the rope while I steer Tallas back to the ranch?" he asked.

I had never towed a tornado anywhere, so to say yes would have been a lie. I shrugged my shoulders and said, "I'll give it a try?"

With a sudden jolt, we took off across the plains toward the ranch. Tallas galloped slower now that he was tugging a tornado behind him. The tornado had a good pull on the rope, forcing me to hunch over Tallas's haunches. This was my chance to ask Dexas more questions about Grandpa.

Dexas said Grandpa came to him the day he vanished and said he was on the tail of whatever caused the time change. The two of them spent some time searching for tornadoes, but not just any tornado. Grandpa was looking for a specific twister: large, black, and more powerful than the average one.

That day they caught twenty, but none was the one Grandpa was looking for.

"Then, on the way back to the ranch, just as we were about to call it a day, something caught your grandfather's eye. A beastly twister descended. It took the two of us and Tallas to surround it. With the combination of our two ropes, we were able to bring it in. Keeping it in the pen, though, has been dangerous, but I promised your grandfather I would hold on to it."

"Stoker?" I asked.

"Yep, that mean ol' thing has been tough to keep. It's taken at least thirty of the twisters I've caught, but I'll do whatever it takes to keep it. Your grandfather wouldn't have asked me if it wasn't important."

"Did he tell you why he wanted that particular tornado?" I asked.

"Nope. He said the less I knew the better. I'm not a man of many words, so I just accepted the job and wished him the best."

We reached the ranch and approached the gate. The other tornadoes stood still, as if they were watching us and waiting to see who the new twister was. Dexas hopped off Tallas and opened the pen. Tallas needed no instruction and trotted into the pen on his own. I held on tight to the tornado.

"I'm gonna close the gate!" Dexas shouted.

The tornado had calmed since we caught it, almost like it had accepted defeat. I loosened my grip and jumped off Tallas. When I landed, a few of the other tornadoes scattered. I thought I might have scared them, but then I saw Stoker charging right at me like a freight train.

I dove out of its direct path and grabbed Tallas, who dragged me off to the side. Dexas was thrown backward as Stoker plowed through the open gate, bending the steel like paper.

By the time Dexas got to his feet and helped me up, Stoker was a couple of miles away. Tallas stood alert next to the fence.

"You all right?" Dexas asked.

"I think so. You?"

Dexas brushed his face, and blood smeared across his brow. "I'll be fine. Just a few cuts."

He ran to the newly captured tornado and released his rope. "Hop on Tallas. I'm going to tie off the gate, and we'll go after Stoker," he said.

Dexas fastened a smaller spare rope around the bent gate and joined me on top of Tallas.

"That should hold it for now. Heeyah!" he shouted, and Tallas took off running faster than before. It felt like we were flying. Grass and dust sprayed beneath our feet with every stride. The clouds above swirled and moved in the same direction as Stoker.

Soon Stoker was in sight. Without any direction from Dexas, Tallas swung wide to cut the tornado off at a safe distance. A showdown had begun, and we took turns charging each other.

Stoker stopped abruptly, and we rode ahead and turned to face it head-on. Dexas pulled the reins, and when Tallas stopped, he jumped off and twirled his lasso.

"I'm going to need your help, Alden," he said without taking his eyes off Stoker.

"Are you kidding? I've never done this before! I'll get killed!" I shouted so he could hear me above the swirling wind.

"You'll do just fine. Just follow my directions and no one will get hurt, not even the tornado—well, okay, the tornado a little bit, but you'll be fine."

"No, I won't!" I shook my head.

"Trust me, you'll be okay. I'll guide you the whole way. There's nothing to fear!"

This was a do-or-die moment, and surely I was going to die. I was a cautious, planning kind of kid. I would never try to wrangle a tornado without months, maybe even years, of practice. Now, in a matter of minutes, Dexas expected me to just follow his lead and wing it. But what was I going to do? We were in an open field with nothing around us for miles.

I closed my eyes and pictured Grandpa with me. He'd wrangled tornadoes before. He'd even helped capture this same tornado. I had to do it for him. This was the tornado he wanted, and if I didn't do this now, I might never know why he wanted it.

I opened my eyes and took a deep breath. "Okay, what do I have to do?" I asked.

"I want you to hold your arms out wide and walk along the right side."

I didn't understand how holding my arms out wide made much sense, but I assumed this was a way of making myself appear larger and possibly more threatening much like one might do in an attempt to scare off a wild animal.

"I'm going to take the left, and Tallas will stand ahead of it!" shouted Dexas.

A quick gust of wind blew in my direction and knocked me down.

"Woo-hoo! You want to play rough, do ya!" Dexas shouted.

I got up and brushed the dirt off my clothes. My right leg, which had been bothering me since Stoker's first charge, throbbed and burned. It felt like it was on fire.

"You okay? We're going to bull-rush it!" Dexas shouted from the other side.

"Bull-rush it? What does that mean?" I shouted, and I rubbed my leg furiously.

Suddenly another burst of wind knocked me down and sent me stumbling. I got back up and the pain in my leg intensified.

"You okay? On my count of three!" he shouted back.

As Dexas started the count, I couldn't stop rubbing my leg. The pain was unbearable.

"One..."

I reached into my pocket to massage my leg and felt something hot against my fingers. I pulled Grandpa's notebook out. The rope was glowing and sparking as if it was on fire.

"Two..."

The rope unraveled, began spinning wildly, and released the notebook from its grip.

"Three! Go!"

Dexas's rope and Grandpa's rope shot toward Stoker and secured themselves tightly around the tornado's midsection. The ropes squeezed tighter as Stoker bucked and tried to break free.

Dexas struggled to grip his rope as he looked at me. "What was that?"

"I don't know! It unraveled and threw itself!" The end of the rope still glowed and sparked in my grip. "It just about burned my leg off before I noticed it!"

Then Dexas's rope twisted and snapped off, throwing Dexas backward onto the ground. I realized then that I was the only one holding the twister in place.

"I've never seen any rope do that before. It's glowing!" Dexas shouted.

"What are you talking about? You told me you've done this before, so what do you mean you've never seen any rope do that before?" I said.

"I've never seen a rope do that before. It just doubled—and that glow! It was glowing! It's still glowing!" he said.

The rope wrapped itself tighter around the middle of Stoker, and the tornado bulged at its top and bottom. Finally, the middle burst and a wave of misty rain exploded across the plain, knocking us down.

We both got up and looked where the tornado had just been. Grandpa's rope still glowed and was knotted in the middle.

"I've never seen a rope dissipate a tornado on its own before," Dexas said.

Dexas stood there, shocked. His rope had already settled back on his arm. I followed Grandpa's rope toward the center and worked on the knot. A shiny silver object the size of my hand fell to the ground when I loosened the knot.

The object was in the shape of a half moon, round on one side with a long silver stick at the top. The half circle appeared to have been created by snapping it off another half. I searched the ground for other pieces, but I found nothing.

"What is it?" Dexas asked.

"I don't know, but it looks broken," I said, turning the object in my hand.

"It looks like your grandfather might have adjusted that rope," he said, pointing to the glowing lasso.

"C'mon, I've got a bag on Tallas and you can put all that stuff in it and we'll head back to the ranch." He pointed to the collection of objects on the ground: the glowing rope, the silver circle, and Grandpa's notebook. I checked my other pocket just to make sure the Lantern of Ayla and my pocket watch were still there. I heard them clang against each other. It was amazing I was able to walk with my collection of trinkets weighing down my pants.

"Dexas, now that the rope is off of the notebook, I can see what Grandpa wrote in it!" I shouted from behind him on Tallas's back.

THE NOTEBOOK

Back at the ranch, the other tornadoes seemed almost jubilant now that Stoker was gone. They danced around each other, and even Dusty got in on the action and twirled between the larger twisters.

Dexas showed me to the water trough, and we washed the dirt from our faces. I reflected on defeating Stoker, and I felt powerful. I felt like I could do anything.

After washing, we gave Tallas a bucket of hay and grains, and Dexas made a fire. I had been there all day, yet the light had never changed. The sky was filled with clouds and looked like it was on the verge of dusk. I never asked Dexas, but I assumed the time change had cast the Pelted Plains into a constant state of twilight.

Dexas removed the satchel from Tallas's saddle and threw it in my lap. "There you go. Open the notebook and let's see what it says."

I pulled back the flap and removed the glowing rope, the silver object, and the notebook. Dexas picked up the glowing rope and examined it a little closer, and I opened the notebook.

The pages were filled with stories and drawings. Grandpa's handwriting spread to the edges of the pages and left no space empty. I could have easily spent hours reading through it all, but toward the back of the notebook I found a series of images that looked similar to the silver object. The drawings displayed a grandfather clock, like the one in the Time Table, a pendulum, and that same pendulum broken into two pieces.

I picked up the silver piece from the tornado and held it up to the drawing. It looked like the right half of the pendulum. The text beneath the drawings explained a theory for the time change: the pendulum had been stolen and broken into two pieces, causing an epic shift in the timelines of every story. A fake pendulum was placed in the Grandfather Clock to avoid any suspicion. A man with no eyes hid the pieces of the pendulum: one in a horrific tornado and another in a place called the Banshee Burrows.

The last page of the notebook stated that the replacement pendulum was actually stealing time from writers, rapidly depleting time from their stories and the characters that inhabited them. The last two paragraphs were the most unnerving: they said death came at a much faster pace for writers in the real world. Fellow writers died from fast-moving diseases such as cancer.

I was familiar with that word, *cancer*. In my quest to learn more about Grandpa's disappearance and the cause of the time change, I had almost forgotten about my father's disease. Was it just a coincidence that my father was suffering from a disease Grandpa wrote was taking writers' lives? Millions of people died from similar diseases, and surely not all of them were writers like Grandpa and me.

As far as I knew, my father wasn't a writer and had no magic abilities. Maybe the time change had begun affecting the family members of writers?

Dexas looked at me in disbelief. "Your grandfather never mentioned any of this to me."

"Maybe he was trying to protect you. Maybe he thought he could save everyone, so there was no need to get everyone worked up," I said. I scanned the page again and saw another mention of the Banshee Burrows. "Did Grandpa ever mention this place to you?"

"No, but like you said, maybe there was no need to mention it."

I skimmed the notebook again and looked for any information on the Banshee Burrows, and near the middle I found a page with it in the title. It was described as a haunted place deep within the woods. Dark fairies with large glowing eyes called banshees screamed and howled in the dark when death was near, and they lived deep underground.

The Banshee Burrows sounded a lot like the place in the woods of *The Lonely Tree.*

I had to go.

I closed the notebook and stood up. "Dexas, I have to find this place. I have to find the other piece of the pendulum."

"I understand," he said, and he handed me the satchel. "Take this and put all your stuff in it."

I placed the rope, the broken piece of the pendulum, and the notebook in the satchel and threw it over my shoulder.

"Any chance you want to come with me?"

After I put the invitation out there, I realized I had no idea how Dexas would get to the Banshee Burrows. Could he hold on to the writing table? Would he be able to travel there on his own? He said he had never heard of the place before, and it's not like I had an address to give him.

"Thanks for the invite, son, but I can't travel to other worlds written by writers unless the author writes me in it."

"Oh, I see."

"C'mon, I'll take you back to the table," Dexas said.

We mounted Tallas and set off toward the writing table. As we galloped, my feeling of empowerment slipped away. I would have to go to the Banshee Burrows alone to find the other piece of the pendulum.

When we arrived at the writing table, Dexas turned to me and said, "Now don't go gettin' all worried about them Burrows. Just remember, you got that glowing rope, and if it performs anything like it did with Stoker, then it's not you who should be worried."

Although I hadn't known Dexas for very long, my departure from him felt glum.

"Dexas, do you get many visitors?"

"No, sir, just your grandpa, but that's all right. I like being one with nature."

It was on his last phrase that I remembered my father. "Being one with nature" was what my father always said, and after leaving him the other night, I wondered how long I had been gone.

Dexas tipped his hat, and when he turned to leave, a tornado blew down and he sped off after it.

THE NOTEBOOK

⋆ ⋆ ⋆

Dexas had reminded me of my father, and after visiting the Time Table and the Pelted Plains, I felt I needed to at least check in with my parents before my excursion to the Banshee Burrows.

Back in the loft, I sat at the writing table for a few minutes and thought about all the new information I had. The satchel, the pendulum, and the Lantern of Ayla were gone, and only the rope, the notebook, and the pocket watch remained. I panicked and thought I might have dropped the pendulum, but I recalled the same thing had happened with the Lantern of Ayla.

Why did some objects come back with me, but others remained in the stories?

With Grandpa's notebook, however, I had a big piece of the puzzle: I needed to find out if my father had the same abilities as me and if he knew anything about the writing table's magic qualities.

I felt like I had been gone for days, and when I entered through the backdoor of my house with the notebook and pocket watch in hand, I wondered if that were true. The house was quiet and empty. The kitchen was dark and showed no signs of dinner, which was what my parents said they were preparing when I last saw them. I walked through the halls and went into every room, but no one was home.

I picked up the phone and called my mother's mobile phone.

"Hello?" she said.

"Mom, where are you guys? I thought you were making dinner?"

"Alden!" she screamed.

"What?"

131

"Where have you been?"

"I…"

I didn't have a story in mind. I hadn't prepared a solid reason for my absence.

"Oh never mind," my mother said. "Tell Mr. Brevard to bring you to the hospital right away."

"Tell Mr. Brevard? And why do I need to come to the hospital?"

"Didn't he tell you?"

"Tell me what?"

"Mr. Brevard. Is he not there with you?"

Both of our voices rose with confusion.

"No, there is no one here, and why would he be here?"

"Don't go anywhere! I'll call you right back," she said.

"Where would I go? Hello—Mom?"

She hung up on me, and I stood in front of the phone, trying to piece together what little information I'd gathered from the call.

A few moments later, the phone rang. I picked it up, and my mother explained that Mr. Brevard was on his way over. I heard a loud beeping noise through the phone and a commotion of voices.

"Alden, I have to go. Hurry and get here."

The line went silent, and I hung up the phone. I didn't have to wait long for Mr. Brevard. I was startled when the door opened and he stood on my front porch.

"What's going on?" I asked.

Mr. Brevard explained I had been gone for hours, and my father's cold had rapidly progressed into pneumonia and he was in the hospital.

I had lost track of time between the Time Table and the Pelted Plains. My parents must have been sick with worry about me. How could my father's health have declined so quickly?

During the car ride to the hospital, Mr. Brevard explained that he knew about the writing table and its magic. After I had gone missing, my mother called him, wondering if he knew where I was.

Although Mr. Brevard had not been around the house much since Grandpa's disappearance, he was still a close friend of the family and my teacher. My mother thought he might know my whereabouts, since she recalled my father telling her I was in the loft working on an assignment for his class. I had forgotten the lie I told my father before traveling to the Time Table. Mr. Brevard offered to come to the house to wait for my return.

"Alden, I found this in the loft when I was looking for you."

From the pocket inside his jacket, Mr. Brevard pulled the small black metal journal with the chapter titled "The Time Table."

"It was Grandpa's. Did you read it?" I asked him.

He glanced at me, and there was a long pause as if we both wanted to ask each other a question but didn't know the best way to ask it.

"I read the chapter that was opened," he said.

I wasn't sure whether to ask him if he knew about Grandpa and his magical writing table. If he didn't know, would I just sound crazy? How could I rebound from such a question?

"Grandpa was a pretty good writer, huh?" I responded.

"Alden, I'm going to ask you something strange, but I hope you don't think I'm too weird for asking."

"You know, don't you? You know about the writing table and grandpa's powers, don't you?" The words rushed from my mouth.

"I had a hunch you were one of us when I first gave out the assignment, and yes, I know about your grandpa's special abilities with the writing table. Were you using the writing table? Did you go to the Time Table? Is that where you have been?"

I was relieved to finally have someone from my world to talk to about it all, but I was also shocked to learn that my fifth-grade teacher was a writer like me.

"Yes—well, I started there and then got sidetracked. How did you know about Grandpa's abilities? Did he tell you?"

"Well, sort of—before I started teaching, I took his classes at the university. He took an interest in me. He said the way I told stories reminded him of his own writing. He said I had the ability to really capture the scene, with details that made my story sound like I had actually been there living it. I was feeling confident one day when I asked Colvin how he knew I hadn't actually been to these worlds I wrote about. I said this right before he handed me back a story I turned in for an assignment called 'The Time Table.'"

I couldn't believe it. Mr. Brevard was a writer like Grandpa. A writer like me.

"There was no denying our shared ability after that story I turned in."

Mr. Brevard's confession made me feel not so alone anymore. I hoped I might elicit his help to fix the time change.

"Your father caught pneumonia, and the doctors are trying to help him. How much time is on your watch?" he asked.

I had forgotten about the watch. "I don't know. It doesn't seem to be working."

"The same thing happened to me, and I think I know why."

He removed a similar pocket watch from his jacket. His watch looked just as old as mine. It was an aged bronze with similar scuff-marks, as if it too had been around for hundreds of years. "I think our watches are protecting us—"

He didn't have to finish. "—from tainted time," I said. "Grandpa wrote in this notebook that the pendulum in the Grandfather Clock is a fake and it's taking time from us."

"Our watches have old magic that prevents anyone from tampering with them. Whatever it is that's doing it is a mystery to your grandpa, and me, but my time is running out. I was lucky enough to have filled it before your grandpa informed me."

"At least you have time. Mine doesn't have any."

I handed my watch to Mr. Brevard.

"That can't be." His eyes diverted from the road to the watch and then back to the road.

"But how—" Mr. Brevard started.

"I know. Nobody knows how it's possible I have no time on my watch yet I'm still here."

"That's impossible!" Mr. Brevard insisted.

I decided to turn the subject back to Grandpa's journal.

"We need to figure out how to fix the time change, and I think I found the answer in Grandpa's journal here."

I opened the rope-bound journal and read the text to Mr. Brevard.

"Grandpa wrote that the pendulum had been broken in half and replaced with a replica that takes time away from writers. I found one piece, and I think I know where the other one is."

"So that's why so many of us are dying and our worlds are crumbling. Without the real pendulum, the Clock can't give us real time. How could the Time Table not know, though?" he asked.

"They know. At least, I think the Master Timekeeper knows. I found documents at the registrar's office that show hundreds of records of writers claiming their time was taken, but no one has been told about it—not even their staff."

"Let's discuss in a few minutes after we've checked on your mother and father."

We arrived at the hospital, and my father's situation was direr than Mr. Brevard had led on. Frail and unconscious, he was hooked up to beeping machines. My mother hugged me as soon as she saw me and cried uncontrollably. I cried too, shaken by the reality of my father's health. I wondered if I would ever be able to talk to him again.

After my mother and I spent some time together, I walked into the hall and asked Mr. Brevard, "Does my father have the same ability?"

"I don't think so. He never gave me that impression or hinted he knew about the writing table. He was just as distraught as your mother when you disappeared."

Tears swelled at the thought of my parents dealing with yet another lost family member. First Grandpa goes missing and then me. I grabbed Mr. Brevard's arm. "You have to help me fix this! You have to help fix the time change. If I can restore the Grandfather Clock, maybe I can somehow stop my father from dying. I can't lose my father." I was running out of time, even though I had no idea how much time I had left. "The other piece of the pendulum is in the Banshee Burrows. You have to go with me," I said.

Mr. Brevard hesitated and said, "I'm sorry, Alden, but I've never heard of such a place, and if it was written by your grandfather, I can't travel to places written by other writers."

In the heat of the moment, I had forgotten what Dexas told me about characters not being able to travel to other stories. I should have assumed the same rules applied to writers, but then I realized I didn't write about the city of Ayla or the Pelted Plains.

"But that's just it. I didn't write these stories either, but I've been able to travel to Grandpa's stories."

Mr. Brevard stopped me. "Only writers of the same bloodline can travel to each other's stories."

"But you both were able to travel to the Time Table?"

"The Time Table is a communal world. All writers have the ability to go there, since all of our stories are logged in the city."

How was I going to find the other piece of the pendulum and fix the clock in time to save my father and essentially save the fictional world? It was too big a task for a kid like me.

Then I remembered Tula's story of the little girl who stopped the evil man from destroying everything. I remembered chasing Stoker down and all the feelings of *I can't* that resulted in *I can.*

I can do this. I can do this. I repeated it in my head.

"Mr. Brevard, I need to get back to the writing table, but I know my mother isn't going to let me leave. Can you help me?"

"I'm a writer, and stories are my specialty," he said with a smile.

We walked back into my father's room. I hugged my mother tightly.

"Kay, I'm going to take Alden down the hall to get a soda. We'll be right back," Mr. Brevard said. "Can I bring you anything?"

My mother relinquished me from her grip, wiped the tears from her eyes, and dabbed her nose.

"No, I'm fine. Hurry back, though. I want to know where you've been," she said, narrowing her eyes at me.

Mr. Brevard and I walked slowly down the hall and then transitioned into a sprint out the front doors.

"That was the best story you could come up with?" I said jokingly.

Mr. Brevard laughed. "C'mon, we don't have much time before your mom notices how long we've been gone!"

On the car ride home, I planned my next steps with Mr. Brevard. I would go to the Banshee Burrows alone. I would get the other piece of the pendulum, travel to the Time Table, and get Tula to help me restore the Grandfather Clock. This should set the time back to normal and, at the very least, stop the progression of my father's illness. In the back of my mind, I held a spot for the grim reality that all of this was based on a theory. I had no idea if there was anything else that had been manipulated to cause the time change.

Back at the house, I ran to the writing table in the loft. "It's still strange to me you have no time but you're still able to travel to your stories," Mr. Brevard said.

I placed the rope and the notebook on the table. "I've wondered the same thing."

I opened Grandpa's journal and began reading about the Banshee Burrows. The room exploded with light, and I was on my way.

THE BANSHEE BURROWS

With Grandpa's detailed story of the Banshee Burrows, I was able to land much deeper in the forest than when I first arrived in Ayla City. As soon as I arrived, I heard cries coming from all directions. Each one sounded slightly different than the others. One sounded like someone yelling, another sounded like a moan, and then there were the more frightening ones, the screams that sounded like someone was being tortured.

On top of the writing table sat my collection of objects: the satchel, the Lantern of Ayla, the notebook, the rope, my pocket watch, and the pendulum. I put everything in the satchel and made my way through the forest. Although the lantern would have lit the way, I wasn't ready to alert anyone or anything to my presence, so I moved slowly and cautiously through the dark.

Grandpa's notebook mentioned a banshee named Gueulard, so my plan was to find her. *How* I was going to find her was the question. I followed a path between rows of trees and looked for anything that might point me in the right direction. A full moon provided a little light, but I was mostly in pure darkness.

The farther I crept through the forest, the more the branches created a thick canopy, the darker the forest became, and the more I kept bumping into things. Soon my eyes adjusted to the near darkness. I was about to concede and use the Lantern of Ayla when tiny specks of light appeared all over the surrounding tree trunks. I approached a cluster and saw hundreds of little windows. Large, furry, blue caterpillars inched their way into tiny chairs and read miniature books inside the trees.

They were all reading. When they finished one book, another book would appear. One caterpillar crawled into a pink velvet chair. It read a tiny book by the light of the smallest lamp ever made. Perhaps they were bookworms? Their cuteness softened the scariness of the forest, and I thought perhaps this trip wouldn't be as horrible as I'd first thought.

But then, a few trees over, I heard a buzzing sound and saw a fairy-like girl reach into one of the openings, draw a bookworm from its chair, and eat it. And then she did it again. Her wings fluttered like a hummingbird as she hovered and pecked at the bookworms with long, bony fingers.

I crouched, in fear she would see me, but she was too busy eating. She let out an abrupt scream, and bits of bookworm sprayed a nearby tree. It startled me, and I fell backward and crushed a few branches. She fluttered toward me and hovered inches from my face. Her eyes glowed green, and I found them alarming but enchanting.

"Who are you?" she hissed.

"I'm…I'm…Alden," I stuttered.

She examined me and fluttered forward and backward as if to understand me from all angles.

"Why are you here?" she asked.

"I'm…I'm looking for Gueulard."

"What do you want with her?" she asked.

I couldn't stop staring into her eyes. I wondered if she was swirling about me or if I was swirling about her.

"I need to talk to her," I said. I thought it best to keep as many details to myself, since the fairy did not initially present herself in a trusting manner, the way she snatched the bookworms from their homes and ate them.

She circled me again and screamed toward the sky.

"Can you tell me where I can find her?" I asked after she stopped yelling.

She looked at me, and then ate a few more bookworms. I begged her to tell me where Gueulard was. She just stared blankly.

"Can you please tell me where I can find her? I promise to leave you alone if you can just point me in the right direction."

She pinched a few more worms and then flew behind me and grabbed the back of my shirt.

"I'll take you to her," she hissed.

She lifted me off the ground, and we swiftly made our way through the forest. We weaved in between the pine trees, and with each turn I was sure she was going to throw me smack into a tree trunk. Below, I could see thousands of bookworms lighting up tree branches like a net of lights on a Christmas evergreen. In a swift lift toward the sky, the fairy carried me high above the trees. I screamed with fear, as we had to be as high as airplanes in the sky.

The fairy shook me and screeched, "Quiet or I'll drop you!"

I tried to calm myself by looking straight ahead rather than at the trees beneath my dangling feet, their branches protruding from the taut pines, sure to impale me should I fall. My nerves subsided as I saw an enormous white moon floating in the distant sky next to a snow-covered mountain. There was not a single cloud in sight. The moon's glow covered the treetops and illuminated the bright white snow that cascaded down the mountain's peak.

Just as sudden as before, the fairy quickly dropped back into the forest. The air got colder, and the darkness thickened. Despite the moon's powerful glow, it was no match for the dense woods overhead.

The fairy's eyes acted like a flashlight and lit the path in front of us. We came upon a vast cave surrounded by dirt. To the left and right, similar caves formed a city of dark openings. More fairies fluttered in and out of the caves. Every now and then one would let out an ear-piercing, startling scream. All of their glowing eyes cast a subdued glow around me.

"This is her burrow," the fairy said, pointing to the abyss in front of me.

The burrow looked like the opening to a trapdoor spider's home. I expected something to jolt out of the opening and pull me in. I nodded to the fairy and walked hesitantly into the burrow.

Smells of tree moss, dirt, and stale air wafted toward me, and my heart beat louder. I wanted to let out one of those horrific screams. As I continued my descent into complete darkness, the cold air became more frigid and my teeth chattered.

I heard a buzzing sound, like the low hum that came from the fairy who brought me to Gueulard's burrow and like the one that chased me on my way to Ayla City.

"Hello?" I asked.

A pair of green eyes glistened inches in front of me. I jumped back, startled.

"Who are you, and what do you want?" a woman's voice said.

I was surprised at how close she was to me, but I managed to say, "My name is Alden, and I found your name in my grandpa's notebook. Colvin Rowe. I was wondering if you could help me?"

The buzzing sound floated from one side of the burrow to the next and back and forth.

"Are you Gueulard? A fairy told me she lived here," I said.

The green eyes bolted forward, and I fell backward to the ground. My pocket watch tumbled out onto the dirt.

"We are not fairies! We are banshees!" she seethed. Her tone then changed to a pout, almost as if she was crying, "I'm Gueulard."

She let loose a sniffled cry and then screamed.

I grabbed my pocket watch and placed it back in the satchel. I then stood and brushed the dirt off my pants.

"Why do you keep screaming?" I asked.

"It's what we do. We scream when death is near—when death is approaching those around us."

I swallowed a hard gulp.

"I'm looking for the other half of this." I removed the broken pendulum from the satchel and held it in front of me. The silver surface reflected in her eyes.

"Where did you find that?" she asked in a raspy voice.

"Can you tell me where the other piece is?" I asked, ignoring her question.

She emerged from the darkness, fluttered in a circle, and stared me down. "You must hide it or he will find you," she said in a changed, panicked voice. She sniffled again and cried. "Please go. He will find you."

"Who will find me?"

She charged at me. "The Macabre!" she wheezed.

Her crying continued. "He made me keep the other piece you seek."

I didn't understand. I remembered the Macabre from the story of the Guardians of Twelve, but he was supposedly destroyed by the little girl—or was he? I couldn't remember if he was destroyed, or did he just disappear? I didn't have time to figure that story out. I needed the other piece of the pendulum, and Gueulard had it.

"Please give me the other piece!" I exclaimed.

The crying stopped, and she fluttered slowly toward me again. In a monotone voice, she said, "He will destroy you should you defy him. He nearly killed all of us the last time your grandfather came here."

"What do you mean?"

She sank to the ground, and a small light emitted from her. She sat hunched over and cried. The light inside her grew brighter.

She was a sprite of a girl, with thin, long white hair and white strands of fabric covering her frail and emaciated body. Her skin was a pale, muted gray. The skin on her face was wrinkled like an old woman's hand, splotchy and discolored with deep purple bruises. Her wings were long and slender. Although both wings were perfectly proportioned, they both had matching tattered edges that looked like something had torn them in the exact same spot.

"He cursed us! Or most of us, anyway. The ones he didn't curse he took with him. Killed them. He took our combs, and with them our beauty." Her eyes filled with tears.

"Your combs?" I asked softly.

Gueulard explained she had not always been a screaming banshee. She and her sisters used to sing beautiful songs when death came for the living. They had been charming spirits who maintained their beauty by using magical combs to brush their hair. The brushes were used to keep the darker parts of death from seeping into their souls. With each stroke they removed all the negative energy that desperately tried to cling to them.

With the magic of the combs, they paraded around those on the brink of crossing into the next world. Their delightful voices were a warm welcome for the recently departed. Some of the banshees would even wash the bloodstained clothing of war-torn soldiers so their journey into the afterlife would be a clean and new start.

Their inviting music echoed throughout the land when they lived at the top of the mountain, which contained a platform for people before sending the dead onto the heavens.

All was lost, though, when the Macabre came and took their combs, allowing the hideous parts of death to strip them of their elegance. Their calm, melodic voices turned into tearful shrieks and chained them to the gloomy depths of the cold and damp underground burrows. Their home at the top of the mountain was buried in a thick ridge of snow, and the dead were only sent to be with the Macabre.

For the banshees that were left behind, the Macabre cursed them to an eternal life of servitude. They would remain in the aphotic burrows under his control forever.

"A lot of strange things happened when this pendulum was broken. Maybe we can restore all that has been changed by piecing the pendulum back together," I said.

The green slits of her eyes dimmed.

I felt sorrier for her than fearful. She was just a little girl who lost her family to the wickedness of the Macabre. I walked toward her to offer comfort, but she looked at me and let out a horrendous, tortured shrill. She flew at me and snatched the silver pendulum piece from my hands, and before I could do anything, she took off toward the entrance of the burrow.

"Stop!" I yelled as I chased her. Her glow lit the path back out.

When she reached the opening, she flew toward the sky. I quickly rummaged through my satchel and pulled out the glowing lasso. I gave it a few twirls and threw it toward Gueulard. The rope wrapped around her waist, and I began reeling it in.

"Let me go!" she spat.

"Not until you give me that piece of the pendulum and tell me where I can find the other one!" I yelled back.

Even after I had gotten her to the ground, she refused to release the pendulum. The rope began to tighten, just as it had with the unyielding tornado.

"Gueulard, if you don't give me that piece of the pendulum, this rope will cut you in half!"

She squirmed, and the rope got even tighter.

"Gueulard, please! I need it to restore time and save my father from dying!"

She dropped the pendulum piece, and the rope released her. She fell to her knees and started crying. I couldn't tell if she was being genuine or if she was trying to trick me again. I quickly grabbed the piece of the pendulum she had stolen from me.

"Gueulard, where can I find the other piece? Please tell me before it's too late!"

Through her tears, she whispered, "The Macabre has it. He came back for it not too long ago and said it would be safer with him."

She looked up at me. Her eyes were swollen from crying and her face chapped from tears that had dried on her cheeks. New tears swelled in her eyes and took dried flakes of the previous ones as they rolled off her face and fell to the ground. I had never seen someone look as defeated as Gueulard.

"I'll take you to him," she said.

I expected her to grab my shirt and take flight just as the previous banshee had done, but instead she chose to walk with me back to the writing table, her eyes lighting the path ahead.

For the first few minutes we walked in repose, but the deathlike silence with the occasional distant scream kept spooking me, so I felt it was necessary to inquire more about how Grandpa encountered her and her life as a banshee.

"How did you meet my grandpa?"

"I was flying through the forest one afternoon when I heard the sound of a man crying. The sound came from a part of the forest I could not recall ever being in. Sitting in the middle of a voluminous field of lavender, a man was wiping the tears from his eyes. His hair was as white as porcelain and he looked like a pearl in the mouth of an oyster. He stared at me with bewilderment among the lavender that was the most vivid purple I had ever seen. The light that crept through the surrounding trees made the violet swell in my eyes."

Grandpa's thick alabaster hair was one of his most prominent attributes, and my parents frequently made references that they hoped we all aged with a woolly head of hair like Grandpa.

"I approached your grandfather assuming he had just passed away because only the dead can see and interact with banshees and he was confused about where he was. I explained that I was a banshee and I was there to help him pass into the next world. He kept looking at me as if I was the strangest thing he had ever seen, but I suppose for most people that is normal."

Gueulard abruptly let out one of her screams, startling me. She was right about Grandpa, though. The sight of a flying banshee with large, glowing eyes was not something he would have been used to seeing. What sparked my attention the most was that Gueulard said only the dead can see banshees.

"You said only the dead can see you?"

"Well, it was what I thought until your grandfather presented his pocket watch."

"You know about the pocket watch?"

Gueulard looked at me with assurance. It was the kind of confidence that made me feel ridiculous for even thinking she was not aware of how her world was created and the life of her maker.

"When I saw the pocket watch, I recognized it as the same one that was once owned by a man named Vincent Rowe. Your great-grandfather."

I tried to recall any memory of my great-grandfather, in conversation or perhaps a picture I might have come across, but nothing triggered any recollection of that name or who he was.

"When I saw that watch, I knew your grandfather wasn't dead. I knew he wasn't dead because he held the same watch as Vincent and it's the same one I saw fall out of your bag back in the burrow."

I reached in the satchel and pulled out the pocket watch. I examined it as if rereading the history of my family, just as Gueulard had explained.

"Did Grandpa say why he was crying?"

"He said he just lost someone close to him."

"It was his father, Vincent, wasn't it?"

Gueulard nodded. "Your grandpa agreed to keep our world alive, and although time has always been granted to us, he rarely came to visit, and just a few years ago he stopped coming altogether."

"Why did the Macabre ask you to keep the other piece of the pendulum?"

"He thought the pendulum would never be found if we kept it because it isn't possible for anyone alive to encounter us. Only the dead can see and interact with banshees, and to make our presence even more sour and repelling, he took away our beauty and song. But then he came back for it a few days ago with no explanation."

As we walked, I noticed the back of Gueulard's dress was stiffer than the rest. With each step she took, something teetered in and out of the fabric. Whatever it was, it matched her dress so perfectly that it camouflaged the object.

Gueulard saw I was staring at the object and stopped walking.

"You see it, don't you?" she asked.

"I think I do. What is it?"

She grabbed the wide piece of fabric behind her and spun it around, her grip revealing the object's solid thickness.

"This is my spinto."

She pressed a small button on the side of the rectangular object. Two triangular pieces emerged from the top and bottom and revealed a bow.

Gueulard moved toward a part of the forest where some of the moonlight peeked through the trees. When the light hit the bow, it vibrated with a white glow. In the light I saw it was made of ivory.

"Where's the string?" I asked. The bowstring connecting the top and bottom nocks was missing.

She pulled a single strand of hair from her head and looped each end to the ends of the bow. Once the hair was threaded at each end, it vibrated with the same glow as the bow. The hair thickened and became more visible.

"And the arrow?" I asked.

"We don't use arrows."

"Well, what do you use?"

Gueulard reached to her side as if she was searching her pocket, a pocket that was invisible to me. She opened her palm and presented a round item the size of a quarter and hollow in the middle like a ring. The object had a row of spikes that were short and black around the circumference.

"It's a spinto stone," she said, holding the ring in front of her and narrowing her gaze as if to scope the tree trunk a few feet ahead.

She then held the bow in front of her and pressed the stone against the string. Slowly she pulled the stone toward her mouth and then let out one of her haunting shrills through the middle of the ring. The stone shot straight ahead, and with a thud I saw the spikes dig into the bark of the tree.

"Whoa! That was awesome!" I said.

"It gets the job done, although when I had my singing voice, I could make the spinto stone go farther and hit multiple targets. I can even adjust the length of the spikes."

She removed the stone from the tree and swung it around her finger, making the spikes grow larger. She stopped when the spikes were the size of a steak knife. By spinning the stone in the opposite direction, she was able to make the spikes smaller again.

"That seems like a pretty impressive weapon to have handy."

"If I had my singing voice, the power of the stone would have sliced that tree in half."

Gueulard moved the bow out of the moonlight and the string turned to ash.

"My hair is not as powerful anymore either. My comb kept my hair strong, removing all negative energy, but now the darkness of death

151

clings to me, making my hair brittle and weak. When the string on the bow is taken out of the light, it succumbs to the darkness and turns to ash."

We continued our walk back to the writing table, and my mind lingered on the combs Gueulard referenced. I wanted to know more about them.

"These combs—what are they made of and how did you get them?"

"The combs are made of ivory from moon moths. Before the Macabre took the combs, our burrows were abundant with moon moths, which are active at night when the moon is at its brightest, hence their name. Each moth has tiny tusks that grow and become thicker with age. These moths can live hundreds of years, and with each full moon their tusks grow larger and stronger."

"Well, if they live hundreds of years, then do you kill them for their tusks?"

Gueulard looked at me with disgust and anger.

"Never! When the moth has lived its life to the fullest, they come to the mountain top to pass on into the heavens and they leave behind their tusks for the banshees as a token of gratitude for helping them cross over."

"Where are the moths now? I haven't seen any, and it's a full moon."

"The moon moths are attracted not just to moonlight but also to the ivory of other moon moths. When the Macabre took the combs made from their tusks, they disappeared from our burrows."

It was at that moment we reached the writing table.

I sat in the chair with my satchel draped over my shoulder, and Gueulard fluttered over the table before landing gently on the top. She then spun the spinto stone around her finger and allowed the spikes to grow back to the size of steak knives.

"When you get there, take the spinto stone. You might need it."

She let the stone stop spinning and plunged it into her stomach. Within seconds, I was in front of a graveyard.

THE MACABRE

Gueulard disappeared and I was alone. Only the spinto stone remained on top of the writing table. A large steel gate that opened on a cemetery full of maple trees loomed ahead of me. The maple leaves, despite being a fall orange, clung to the tree branches—not a single one littered the ground. The tree trunks were thick and their leaves huge.

The graveyard, the cool air, and the orange maple leaves reminded me of Halloween. The surrounding pine trees made me think I was somewhere on the outskirts of the Banshee Burrows. The gravestones and statues looked clean and peaceful.

I approached the gate and shook it. It was locked. As soon as I stopped shaking the gate, something small fluttered to my right and landed on a nearby bush. I moved closer to get a better look. When I was only inches from it, I could see it looked like a butterfly, but something large distended from its head. Could it be a moon moth?

I reached to touch what had to be the tusks when it quickly took flight, spreading its fluffy wings. The moth flew through the bars on the gate and landed on a stone pathway.

The cemetery was surrounded by a fence that looked like it would pierce anyone who attempted to climb over it. I circled the entire graveyard, looking for another entrance, but the front gate was the only way in.

I shook the gate one last time, but it wouldn't budge, and there was no other option but to scale it. With my satchel draped over my shoulder, I placed one foot in an opening and started up the gate. In less than five minutes, I scaled over the top and reached the ground.

Once I was inside the graveyard I followed the moth as it moved along a stone hedge. I hoped it would lead me directly to the hidden piece of the pendulum. A few feet along the path, I heard a swooshing sound, like something large and heavy was rocking back and forth. The moth flew in the direction of the sound to a tall, cylindrical crypt with a skull and crossbones on top of a cross that stuck out of the concrete mass.

As I got closer to the crypt, I realized it was turning, twisting in place, and following my direction of movement. Several moon moths were scattered about the walls of the crypt and the one I followed joined them, their wings pulsating with their every breath. The entrance of the tomb followed me as I rounded the crypt. I stopped a few times and walked in the opposite direction to see if the entryway would continue to follow, and it did. I felt afraid, and goose bumps spread across my arms.

The crypt suddenly moved toward me and I ran back to the gate stopping just short of it realizing I would have to scale it again. I turned around to see if the crypt was still following me.

It trailed me but stopped a few feet away. After a few seconds, the loud swooshing sound started again and the front half of the crypt leisurely crumbled away, disappearing into the ground. As the tomb collapsed, hundreds of moon moths fled the center and fluttered into the sky.

In the center of the crypt I saw it, the source of the sound. A black pendulum swung back and forth in a slow stride. The pendulum had a frosted tint, resembling a mammoth black pearl. Beneath the pendulum were thousands of ivory combs. I knew they had to be the combs stolen from the banshees and that was why so many moon months were inside the crypt.

Rocking ever so calmly on top of the pendulum was a figure cloaked in black fabric that frayed at the end of the sleeves and rim of a cape. One leg was propped on top of the pendulum while the other dangled over the front. I followed the leg to the end where a bony foot wiggled in my direction.

The figure steadily removed its hood and revealed a chilling skeletal face and released a recognizable cackle. My heart beat a thousand miles per hour, and I tried to keep up with my breathing. Could it be the Macabre? It did appear a lot like the skeleton from my class assignment, but I couldn't be certain.

The hollow holes where his eyes should have been were wide; the empty sockets were filled with the blackest of black.

His form changed slightly as he slid off the pendulum. Flesh began to ooze between his bones, and some of it dripped onto the ground. A terrible smell filled the air, and his flesh began falling off in larger clumps that writhed in piles of steaming goo.

The hair on the back of my neck rose again, and more goose bumps formed on my arms. The skeleton smiled wider, showing teeth that looked like chipped pieces of harden clay, brown like the rusted blade of a hand saw.

With every step the skeleton made toward me, I moved backward toward the gate. Soon I could move no farther. I closed my eyes for a brief moment and hoped that I could exit faster than I'd entered.

The skeleton clapped and smirked. He then took the complete form of a rotting corpse with partially decayed hair and clothing that was eaten away by bugs, some of them still clinging to his pants.

I remembered the story of the Macabre and how he took the form of some of our darkest fears. For me, one of them was the living dead, and here before me was one of the most terrifying zombies I had ever imagined. A second cackle reverberated through the graveyard, and it was then I was sure this was the Macabre, the same one from my class assignment. It was the distinct sound described as a menacing cackle in the story of the Guardians of Twelve.

"Many before you have tried scaling that fence, but none were as successful as you. They're all here living with me now, actually—permanently," he said.

"Are you the Macabre?" I asked.

"Yes, but you knew that already."

I didn't see any point in stalling my quest for the pendulum, so I got right to the point.

"Gueulard said you had the other half of the pendulum. Where is it?" I asked.

"We will get to that soon enough," he hissed.

"Why did you break the pendulum?" I asked.

He cocked his head at an angle. "I broke the pendulum and replaced it with one that steals time. The stolen time feeds back to this beauty," he said motioning toward the black pendulum behind him.

"Why are you stealing time?"

"To hurry death for everyone! As people die, they will become part of my army and serve under my control."

With that last word, he held out his bony fingers and rolled them into the palm of his hand, making a closed fist.

"What do you need an army for?"

"Well, I'm only happy when there's sadness. So, to take all of those cheerful stories away, I needed to take away their authors. Without their authors, they have no time, and without time, those delightful worlds will vanish and so will their inhabitants. Soon they'll join me here for a rising unlike any story told before."

"What rising?"

He disappeared into thin air. I pressed my back farther against the gate and squeezed the bars. I felt a puff of air in my right ear. I jumped and turned and saw he was on the other side of the gate. He laughed. He flung his hands apart, and the gate flew open.

"You know, my plan was foolproof until your grandfather got in the way. He saw me hiding one of the pieces in that tornado. I should have never listened to Scatterback. It was foolish to hide the pieces in the stories of your bloodline," he said.

"What does Mr. Scatterback have to do with this?"

"He was the one who suggested hiding a piece in your grandfather's stories, the one with the tornado and the one with those annoyingly loud banshees. He said that woman Tula kept a collection of Rowe books on her desk. I thought it was perfect. With each piece hidden in a different story, it would be impossible to find."

"But why would Scatterback help you? What does he have to gain from all this?"

The Macabre cackled again and began acting like a circus performer. He clapped and did cartwheels. With each flip, clumps of flesh fell to the ground and burst into flames.

"I thought your grandpa would have been smart enough to tell you everything before he sent you to finish what he couldn't."

I became irritated by the continued mystery around everything the Macabre was saying. I didn't have time to stand here and play games.

"Looks like you underestimated Grandpa," I replied with conviction.

"That I did, but it worked in my favor. You see, your grandfather was a foolish man. He never should have created two of you. For being a scrapped storybook character, she was smart to come to me."

"Created two of me? Who is 'she'?"

This made the Macabre giggle with delight. He loved that I was clueless about it all. He allowed just a tiny bit of information out each time, just enough to add to my pile of questions and longing for an answer.

"Oh—he didn't tell you?" he said in a knowing tone, toying with me to get a reaction.

"Your grandfather should have never sent that little girl to the Wastelands yet let *you* live."

"What little girl? The little girl from the Guardians of Twelve?"

The Macabre's grin shrunk back to the center of his mouth.

"So he did tell you?"

The Macabre did a backflip and jumped on top of the black pendulum. He flung back his cape to reveal the other half of the broken pendulum.

"I believe you came looking for this, but no matter. You won't need it after I'm through with you."

I wanted my questions answered, but most importantly I needed the other half of the broken pendulum.

"The little girl's plan worked. Breaking the pendulum led your grandpa to her, and in return she knew you would come looking for him—and with you would follow the Writer's Table. With such a big army, I'll be able to bring death and sadness on a much bigger scale to *your* world."

"Where is Grandpa?" I said with anger.

"With her—in the Wastelands."

What was the connection with the little girl and Grandpa, and what did it have to do with letting me live?

"What does the writing table have to do with all of this?"

"The Writer's Table, true to legend, protects the owner from ever running out of time—"

"But that's not true!" I interrupted but did not feel confident in my response. "Grandpa went to the Time Table to fill his watch often. Why would he do that if his time was infinite?"

"That was the one thing your grandfather *was* smart about. He kept up the appearance of needing time so that no one ever suspected he was in possession of the legendary Writer's Table."

"His writing table is made of wood."

The Macabre threw his head back in laughter, his skull almost unhinged from his neck.

"You're as foolish as your grandpa. You think he would have written you a little better, something he could have improved upon."

Written me a little better? I didn't understand what the Macabre was getting at. I had to focus on getting the other half of the pendulum, but how?

"Beneath that veneer of a table is *the* Writer's Table, and once I've gotten rid of you, it will belong to me."

I tried to remember what all Tula said the Writer's Table was capable of, but my head was so muddied with questions about Grandpa, the little girl, and the pendulum.

"So what are you going to do with the writing table? What use is it to you?"

"You don't know what it can really do. What would I do once all of the world's stories and their writers belonged to me? I'd have an army of death and destruction that would take over one story after another, but then what? What would I be able to do once all the stories were gone? Why not take over *your* world!"

I remembered Tula saying that only the one who possesses all of the objects could bring something from the fictional world into my world.

"You can't bring your army into my world. Not without all twelve of the objects, and you don't have those."

"You see, I don't need to go find all twelve objects because the Writer's Table will bring them all to me. Your grandfather was quite the traveler, and what you don't know is that your grandfather used the Writer's Table to visit each of the twelve objects. And clearly you don't know that the Writer's Table can connect to all its previous locations—and bring anything from those places to me!"

"The Guardians won't allow it."

"The Guardians won't even know how they disappeared. I can bring them here without a single trace and bring whatever I want into your world, just like your grandfather."

"What? What do you mean just like my grandfather?"

The Macabre smiled and let out another cackle. He jumped back off the pendulum and danced in a circle like a circus clown gone mad.

"He really should have written you a little better. I know I would have. Now move aside."

From his pocket the Macabre removed a vial of Tell Tale Solution which I recognized by its purple color, and twisted off the stopper. With a flick of his wrist as if throwing a Frisbee, he expelled the solution toward the writing table.

The oak exterior of the table melted away revealing a shimmering metallic stone writing table.

The solution from the Tell Tale Well revealed the writing table's true identity. If only Tula hadn't used hers in our escape from the registrar's office, I would have known what I had all this time.

"I'm going to make my army, and with the twelve objects I'll finish what I started all those years ago."

The Macabre disappeared again and reappeared by the crypt.

I realized that my lack of understanding about the writing table allowed me to play right into the Macabre's hands. I couldn't let his plans come to fruition. I needed to retrieve the other piece of the pendulum and get the Writer's Table out of there.

"You'll never take the Writer's Table from me!" I shouted.

The Macabre cackled again and performed several more cartwheels.

I took the opportunity to run for the table.

"I won't have to take it from you if you're dead!" he shouted.

As I ran, I removed the spinto stone from my satchel. The Macabre vanished but reappeared next to me and reached out to grab me. I sliced the spinto stone at his hand. A tremendous scream pierced the air, and the Macabre flew backward and vanished. The scream sounded a lot like Gueulard's.

The Macabre reappeared directly between me and the Writer's Table. I swung again with the spinto stone and missed, but it sliced his cheek on the upswing. A ripple of sound exploded from his cheek and pushed the Macabre back several feet, ejecting clumps of flesh from his body. The spinto stone contained the force of Gueulard's screams.

When I reached the table, I threw open the satchel to remove the lasso, but the Macabre was already behind me. He threw me to the ground. Long brown vines snaked out from the surrounding woods and twisted around my ankles and torso.

I slashed at the vines with the spinto stone, and the screams pushed them away, but there were too many and they quickly wrapped around me like a cocoon. The Macabre reappeared in front of the gate. He shook his finger at me and slowly rose in the air.

I thought it was the end. I was going to die despite my efforts to fix everything that had gone wrong. I desperately reached for the spinto stone that was wrapped between one of the vines near my right leg, but the vines squeezed tighter. I imagined this was how the tornado felt in the grips of my lasso, and I wondered if I too would be squeezed to death. I wished Dexas were with me. I was sure with his lasso and mine we could beat the Macabre. I wished Babacan were here too with his lanterns to blind the Macabre. I imagined Tula by my side providing me with bits of information to use against the Macabre. Gueulard could use her spinto, and with our powers combined the Macabre would be no more.

The vines constricted tighter around my body. This was the end. I was on the verge of losing consciousness, my head spinning, when the writer's table exploded with light. I thought the Macabre had won and was bringing the twelve objects to his feet. I blacked out for a moment and came back to the sound of Dexas's voice.

"Get up, buddy. You're all right!" he said.

I stumbled to get back on my feet. Dexas pulled me back near the Writer's Table. The table was still enveloped by the light, and from the center Babacan emerged with at least twenty floating lanterns circling above his head.

After Babacan, Tula appeared with a vial of Tell Tale Solution in her hand. The solution was luminescent and projected rays of purple light across her face. We stood beside each other and formed a half circle. Tallas finished the line at the other end. The Macabre floated in the air in front of us. From behind every tombstone, a dead person clutched the air and broke the earth, rose to his or her feet, and marched toward us.

The Macabre cackled again and smiled with glee. "This will be fun. All five of you will serve me well. Alden, your grandfather would be so proud to know his characters came to try to save you."

The light around the Writer's Table intensified, and a swarm of banshees flew into the air led by Gueulard.

"Don't forget to include us!" Gueulard yelled at the Macabre.

At the end of Gueulard's words, the choir of banshees screamed into the moonlit sky and shot their spinto stones at every risen corpse. The corpses responded and showed off their strength by removing their headstones and tossing them at the closest banshee. The quiet graveyard had erupted into a war zone.

"Why are they throwing gravestones into the sky?" Tula asked.

"They are aiming at the banshees," I responded.

"Banshees?" Tula said.

I remembered that only the dead could see banshees with the exception of Grandpa and me, but there was no time to explain, as a tombstone shot over our heads.

With the zombies occupied with the banshees, the Macabre focused in on the rest of us. Dexas extended his arm, and the lasso came to life. He looked at me and nodded. I took that as a hint to do the same. I removed my own lasso, which immediately glowed. Dexas then looked at Babacan and Tula, and they nodded. The lanterns circling above Babacan moved faster, and within a split second they shot up above the Macabre and exploded with light.

The distraction gave Dexas and me the opportunity to lasso the Macabre. Dexas's rope shot toward him. He dodged it, but my rope was close behind and didn't miss. The Macabre wiggled and squirmed to release himself from my rope, but it only tightened around him. Dexas shot his lasso at the Macabre a second time, and it wrapped itself around him too. I pulled the lasso in and wiped his feet out from under him. Dexas helped me pull him over to the writing table, where Tula closed in and used the dropper to cast Tell Tale Solution over him.

"Now I think you'll be serving *us* well!" said Tula.

"Where's the pendulum?" Dexas demanded.

The Macabre tried to morph into something, but the Tell Tale Solution was too powerful.

"It was at his side," I said as I pulled back part of his cloak.

The Macabre squirmed but was no match for the solution. The pendulum piece appeared as if it has been camouflaged before the Tell Tale Solution kicked in.

I hastily grabbed the piece of the pendulum.

The Macabre's constant squirming made my lasso tighten, and just like with Stoker, the more he squirmed, the tighter the rope squeezed.

"Get back! The rope is going to break him in half!" I yelled.

Everyone backed away, and we could hear the sound of his bones cracking. Every bone the rope came in contact with snapped apart. Just as the rope squeezed the last of the Macabre's midsection, the tail ends of the rope weaved around his head and legs, and with one last squeeze the bones turned into a pile of dust.

We slowly walked toward the pile of ashes, and I picked up the lasso.

"The lasso doesn't take prisoners, does it?" Dexas said.

The chaos around us stopped. The zombies reverted back to lifeless corpses and lay on the ground motionless now that the Macabre was no longer controlling them. Above us the banshees swirled and buzzed with victory.

Gueulard flew to my side.

"Is he dead?"

I nodded then said, "I thought you were dead."

"Remember, the Macabre cursed me to be his eternal servant, so I couldn't die. Now that he is gone, I belong to myself again," Gueulard said.

"Oh—and your combs are over there." I pointed to the pile of rubble around the black pendulum. Gueulard motioned to the other banshees, and they gathered around the combs. They immediately began brushing their hair, and in and instant they surrounded themselves with a blinding light.

When the light diminished, a group of young women stood, their skin as smooth as porcelain, their hair thick and glowing, their wings tapered and sparkling, and their dresses were clean and new. They laughed with ecstasy and held their spintos toward the sky. The moon moths that had scattered made their way back to the banshees and danced among their long lost friends.

I looked back at the writing table.

"How did you guys get here? Did the writing table bring you to me?"

"I was in the middle of dusting my lanterns when I heard your voice, and then all of a sudden an explosion of light appeared in front of me. I thought my lanterns had exploded. I walked through the portal, and oddly some of my lanterns followed me. When I came through, I saw you," said Babacan.

"The Macabre said the Writer's Table tracks the places it's been to. He was going to use it to bring the twelve objects to him and use it to raise an army of death," I said.

I looked over at Tula. She held the Tell Tale Solution tight in her hand.

"I knew it was the Writer's Table! I told you, didn't I?" she said.

I grinned. "You were right, Tula. Now, we have to get the pendulum back to the Time Table."

Gueulard flew back to my side. "Before you leave, we must destroy the Macabre's pendulum," she said.

Gueulard motioned for her sisters to surround the black pendulum. Each banshee aimed her spinto at the pendulum.

"On the count of three, ladies," Gueulard said.

On three, each banshee sung a note into the spinto stone. Unlike the terrible shrill Gueulard used before, their voices sounded beautiful. Their song pulsated toward the pendulum, and with the power of their spinto stones, the pendulum disintegrated.

Everyone watched the pendulum crumble as if it had spontaneously combusted, but I was the only one who saw that the banshees were the ones who made it happen.

"What was that?" Babacan exclaimed.

"The banshees. Only the dead and myself can see them. Grandpa was able to see them too. They used their spintos to destroy the black pendulum."

"What now, Alden?" Dexas asked.

"We need to hurry back to the Time Table so we can fix the real pendulum," I said.

We made our way to the Writer's Table, and together we traveled back to the Time Table.

RESTORATION

When we arrived at the Time Table, I didn't know what to expect. The Macabre had revealed that Mr. Scatterback was partially behind all of this, so we needed to be extra cautious. I asked the banshees to remain by the Writer's Table. I could not explain why I was able to see them, and I was afraid we would encounter others with my same ability, so they remained behind.

We were in the same alley as before, and I saw people moving on the streets. With both pieces of the pendulum in my hand, I ran to the time bank with Tula, Dexas, Tallas, and Babacan. The sun and moon rose and set just as before. Inside, I approached the clock unnoticed. Everyone went about their day as usual. Tallas remained outside and I could hear a crowd of people gathering around him.

I stood before the clock and looked at Tula, waiting for her to tell us how to remove the replica pendulum. I had no experience with the mechanics of a clock, and with this being a magical one, I assumed even someone with experience would have to take a guess. A small, winding staircase made its way to the back of the clock, so I asked Tula, "Do we go up?"

Before I got to the first step, someone shouted from the second-level balcony, "Stop them!"

Mr. Scatterback ordered a pair of security guards to capture us. I ran up the stairs by the clock, pulled out the spinto stone, and adjusted it just enough so the spikes were quite visible and held it in front me.

"Come any closer and I'll use this. Trust me, you don't want to be cut by these blades," I threatened.

The security guards pointed their weapons at us and requested I put the spinto stone away. Those in line were silent, and the people coming into the building paused, motionless, and watched me.

"You're all being fooled by this clock! It's a fake!" I shouted.

I removed the pieces of the pendulum from my satchel with my free hand and held them in the air.

"He's lying!" Mr. Scatterback shouted. "He's trying to destroy our clock just like he's done to the one in his hand."

We were running out of time with each spin of the clock's hands.

"You're mistaken," I said to the crowd.

"This man, Mr. Scatterback, is the one who has deceived you all," I said, pointing to Mr. Scatterback as he made his way down the stairs. "He partnered with the Macabre, a man who has been stealing time from all of you."

Mr. Scatterback narrowed his eyes and gritted his teeth. "Lies!" he shouted.

"It's true!" yelled Tula. "This here proves Mr. Scatterback knew the clock was taking time from all of you but did nothing." She held the stack of complaints.

"They used this fake pendulum to take time away from you in hopes you would die and become part of an army of death," I said. I held the broken pieces even higher. "If we don't fix this clock, we'll all be lost, we'll all die, and our stories will fade away and become a monstrous nightmare."

"This is treason! These people are staging a coup to remove me from office. Arrest them!" Mr. Scatterback shouted.

"You're the one who betrayed your people. You used Grandpa's stories to hide the broken pendulum. You took the stories from Tula's desk and told the Macabre to hide the pendulum pieces in them," I said.

Tula looked furious, knowing that her personal collection of Grandpa's stories were used as a ruse and played a part in the death of so many people when their time was taken from them.

"So why did you do it? What did the Macabre promise you? What did you want so bad that you offered up the lives of everyone to play a part in a death army?" I asked.

"He promised me I would rule all of the fictional worlds while he took over the writers' world."

"He had no intention of letting you rule the fictional world because he planned to destroy it all before taking *my* world," I said.

Mr. Scatterback looked shocked and a little in disbelief.

"You did it all for nothing. You didn't care about any of us. You only cared about yourself," Tula said. She made her way down the staircase.

"Take Mr. Scatterback to one of the holding cells until we can arrange a trip for him to the Wastelands," she commanded the nearby security guards.

Mr. Scatterback spat and yelled as he was dragged away. Tula walked back up the stairs to the back of the clock.

"Can we fix it?" I said, and held out the pieces of the broken pendulum.

"I think so," she said. She took the pieces from my hands.

Tula removed the replica with a few tools from her belt. She took a steel thread and bound the two pieces of the pendulum together. The pieces fused together and emitted a tremendous gold light. As soon as Tula lowered the pendulum into the Grandfather Clock, it tripled in size and spun wildly, illuminating the glass clock with a spectacular show of lights. The crowd gave a collective round of applause.

The teller lines resumed, and people filled their watches. Tula and I ran outside and noticed the quick changing of sun and moon had stopped. Daylight had resumed as normal.

Tula gave me a hug. "Thank you."

"I couldn't have done it without your help. Without those registers, we would have been doomed," I said.

"I can see your head is still swimming with questions. Come back and see me soon, okay?" Tula said.

"I should probably take Dexas, Tallas, Babacan, and the banshees back to their worlds," I said.

Tula nodded in agreement, and Babacan, Dexas, Tallas, and I headed back to the Writer's Table.

The banshees had remained vigilant and unnoticed next to the Writer's Table. They took to the air when they saw us approaching, and Gueulard moved slightly in front.

"Were you able to fix the clock?" she asked.

I looked up at the overhead sun. "I think so. The sun appears to be stabilized. I guess we will know for sure once the sun sets at the projected time."

Dexas and Babacan looked at each other in confusion. "Are you talking to us?" Babacan asked.

Things happened so quickly once we arrived in the Time Table I didn't really explain to the others that the banshees had come with us.

"The banshees. They came with us and have been guarding the Writer's Table."

Babacan looked around the Writer's Table as if hoping to catch a glimpse of one of the banshees, but he of course was not able to see them.

"Gueulard, are you okay if we take you and the others banshees back to the burrows first?" I asked.

"Yes, I think that would be wise, since there are so many of us."

Everyone gathered around the Writer's Table, and within a few seconds, we were in the burrows. Upon our arrival, all of the banshees took to the sky and joined hundreds of other banshees making their way to the top of the mountain.

Gueulard lingered for a moment. "Thanks for your help in finding our combs and restoring our world to the glory it once was."

"No, thank you for helping me find my way to the Macabre. I have to admit I was a little shocked when I thought you killed yourself."

174

"Just remember, Alden, death is never the end but a crossroads to what will become."

She then turned and flew into the sky. Her silhouette gleamed in the face of the moon, resembling a shooting star—a star that had found its place again among the constellations.

Next we went to the Pelted Plains. Dexas hopped onto Tallas and tipped his hat in my direction.

"Thanks, Dexas," I said.

"No problem, Alden. Let me know the next time you want to go catch a tornado. Bring that rope of yours too."

A gust of wind bellowed from the sky. Dexas then turned Tallas and rode off as the sun broke through the clouds overhead.

"Shall we?" Babacan said.

When we arrived in Ayla City, it was still dark. I feared by some weird fate that Babacan's world hadn't been corrected, but within a few seconds, we watched as the sun peeked over the horizon and awoke from its long slumber.

A crowd down by the oceanfront erupted into a glorious cheer. Babacan and I stood in silence and let the beauty of the dawn fill our eyes. With each passing minute, the sky came more alive. When the sun finally rose completely above the horizon, I saw tears in Babacan's eyes.

"Thank you for the Lantern of Ayla," I told him. "It was surprisingly useful in a way I could not have imagined."

"That is the best way to use it. When darkness surprises us, we must find our inner light, and only then do we see our way. You are powerful, Alden. Your grandfather was right to put his faith in you. I believe you have the ability to shape mountains, move oceans, create worlds, and change people."

"I just wish Grandpa was here with me," I said.

"But you see, your grandfather has been with you all this time. We never lose the ones we love. They're always there, listening to us. Did your journey not bring him a little closer to you? Have you not realized the strength within you?" he asked.

He was right. I never stopped thinking about Grandpa. I had learned more about him than I ever knew before. The characters he created were fascinating, compassionate, and trustworthy, and that made me believe they were a direct extension of Grandpa. I never would have known this side of him if it weren't for the Writer's Table.

"Babacan, thank you for sending the floating lanterns in the sky. Without them, I never would have found this city and I never would have learned about you and all of Grandpa's friends."

I paused a moment to let the sun pierce through my eyes.

I handed Babacan the Lantern of Ayla and said good-bye. I then sat at the Writer's Table and thought of home.

THE PAINTER'S BRUSH

When I returned home, it was daylight. Afraid that time had escaped me again, I ran into the house and found Mr. Brevard in the kitchen. I startled him when I burst through the backdoor.

"Oh good, you're back," he said.

"How long was I gone?" I asked.

"Only through the night. I was afraid of what I might have to tell your mother if it turned into days. We should probably get back to the hospital. I told her I brought you home to rest so she wouldn't panic."

There was a brief moment of silence as we both stared at one another.

"Well, are you going to tell me how everything went? Were you able to fix the pendulum?"

"Oh right, sorry. The pendulum is fixed. I only hope it saves Dad."

I was exhausted. The whirlwind of being on a quest across multiple worlds left me a little out of it. I fell asleep during the car ride to the hospital.

When we arrived, I found my mother sitting next to my father, holding his hand. My father's eyes were wide open. A feeding tube prevented him from speaking, but I took the tears that ran down his cheeks and the hand squeezes he gave me as signs that he was happy to see me.

A nurse checked his vitals, and I saw her nod to my mother. My father kept his eyes on me. His alertness had to be a sign he was getting better; I was convinced the restoration of the clock worked and, before long, he would be better. I couldn't wait to tell him about my journey and ask him if Grandpa ever mentioned the magic of the writing table.

"It was touch-and-go there for a while, Alden. It was so strange because one minute he was on a downward spiral and then the next thing we know, he stabilized and he came back around," my mother said as she took my hand.

It had to have been when the clock was restored. I couldn't think of any other explanation.

"I can't wait to see you out of that bed, Jay," Mr. Brevard interjected.

No one felt that way more than me. I wanted to get Dad alone so I could ask him more about the Writer's Table, to see if he too had the same abilities as Grandpa and me.

The nurse finished adjusting my father's fluids. "I'm just going to give him a little something to help him rest," the nurse said, then injected a syringe into my father's IV. "I'll be back in just a bit to check on him."

"Kay, why don't you take a quick break? In fact, why don't you go home for a bit and get a few winks? Alden and I will sit with Jay until you get back," Mr. Brevard suggested.

My mother agreed and gave me a hug before leaving.

"Call me immediately if anything changes," she said. "Make sure you take notes if the doctors come by."

"We will," Mr. Brevard assured my mother.

My father's eyes began to shut, and soon he was asleep.

Mr. Brevard and I sat in nearby chairs, each facing my father keeping our promise to my mother to stand attentive over him while he slept.

"Have you ever heard of the Wastelands?" I bluntly came forward with Mr. Brevard.

"Yes. It's a place where all stories and characters are sent when a writer intentionally discards a portion of a story. Anything banished to this world remains in limbo, never fading completely from existence."

"But why do they not fade away? If existing worlds and characters crumble when an author stops telling their story or stops giving them additional time, how is it that their existence in the Wastelands remains intact?"

Mr. Brevard folded his hands in front of him.

"The Wastelands are fragments of stories that often the writer will repurpose; therefore, recalling on a character or place and changing it slightly, but until the writer brings them back they are stuck there."

"I think that is where Grandpa is."

"That's impossible. Writers can't be sent to the Wastelands. Only characters can inhabit that place. We can't even physically travel there. It's forbidden."

I scooted my chair closer to my father's bed. I held his hand and rested my head against the bed rail. Images of my father awake, painting in the forest, swam through my mind. He sat at his easel in the forest. On the canvas was the lavender field where Grandpa first met Gueulard. As my father turned to look at me, I opened my eyes. When I looked up, my father was awake. Mr. Brevard got up from his chair and sat at the foot of my father's bed.

"Jay, you okay?" he asked.

The machines started beeping, alerting the nurse down the hall. Mr. Brevard pressed the call button for the nurse, but she had just entered the room. She checked the machines and noticed my father was awake and signaling something.

"What's going on, Jay?" the nurse asked him.

My father motioned to his feeding tube and made a suggestion to pull it out.

"You want me to take out your feeding tube?" she asked.

He nodded.

She pressed a few buttons on the machine that connected to the feeding tube and then slowly pulled it out.

My father took a deep breath, and after a minute, he spoke in a low, raspy voice, "I saw you in the forest."

"Now don't try and speak, Jay. Your vocal cords will need some time to adjust to you talking again," the nurse said. The nurse then turned her attention to Mr. Brevard and me. "I need to check on another patient but I'll be back shortly."

I thought my dad might have been recalling a previous encounter of us in the woods by our house, but then he said, "Just now in the woods. I saw you—by the purple field."

"Dad, have you ever been able to go to any of the places you've painted?"

Mr. Brevard intensely stared at my father, waiting for him to answer yes.

"What do you mean, Alden?" my father asked.

"Have you ever painted something and it came to life?"

My father looked at me as if it should have been me in the hospital bed.

"What on earth are you going on about?"

"I don't think he has it, Alden," Mr. Brevard said.

"Has what?" my father asked.

There must have been a million ways to better explain what I was asking my father, but thus far the first two did not seem to be working. Perhaps if I explained what happened to me my question would make better sense.

"Dad, what I'm about to tell you may sound crazy, but I want you to just listen and then perhaps my question will be more understandable."

My father looked back at Mr. Brevard. Perhaps he thought that since Mr. Brevard was an adult, he could explain my madness.

"Jay, just listen to him."

"The night before Grandpa disappeared, you read me the book he wrote, *The Lonely Tree*. Something strange happened when I closed my eyes and reimagined the pages in the book. I was suddenly in the book among the illustrations. I couldn't move, but everything around me was moving."

Mr. Brevard sat on the edge of his chair eagerly waiting for me to finish and for my father to make a connection.

"Then two years later I discovered Grandpa's writing table in the loft. I sat at it to complete a writing assignment, and when I imagined the words on my paper, the room exploded into a ball of light and I was transported into the story I had just written. Only this time I could actually move in the story and explore the land as written in my notebook."

My father looked at me and then at Mr. Brevard. He then stared at the wall in silence. I expected him to completely lose his mind at any moment, but instead he said, "Something similar did happen to me once, but I thought I was just tired and imagining things."

"What happened?" I asked.

"I was painting in the woods behind our house—a picture of a squirrel eating something in one of the pine trees. It was hot, and the air was stagnant, but then out of the blue a gust of wind made its way through the forest and the cool air felt so good I closed my eyes for just a moment. In that brief period of time, I imagined my painting, thinking about how to finish it, when abruptly the squirrel came to life and scurried down the tree. It startled me, so I opened my eyes, and there in front of me the squirrel was still in the same place. It hadn't scurried down the tree at all. I thought I had to be losing my mind."

I felt relieved that my father had experienced the same thing I had. I laughed with happiness.

"What's so funny?" my father asked.

"You're like me! We both have the same ability!"

"The same ability to do what?"

I stood up with excitement and then leaned over to give my dad a hug.

"Just you wait until I show you what you can do with your paintings," I said.

Mr. Brevard started laughing too.

"We have to get him home, Alden."

$$\star\ \star\ \star$$

We had to wait two more days before my father was well enough to be discharged from the hospital. The doctors couldn't believe how quickly he had recovered and called it nothing short of a miracle.

The doctors were even more amazed to see the cancer they previously diagnosed him with was completely gone.

Back at the house, my father's strength rapidly returned, and I was finally alone with him in the loft.

"I want you to paint a place we can go to—a place we can visit. Somewhere secluded. It's your first time, and I don't think we should visit a place with a lot of people."

My father positioned a small easel on top of the Writer's Table. He neatly arranged a few jars of paint on the edge of the table and grabbed a large paintbrush from a box on a nearby shelf.

"So what do I do first?" he asked.

"Paint something, and when you're done we will see what happens."

He dipped the brush into the black paint and began to create a cottage. While he painted, I gathered my collection of trinkets I had collected since discovering the Writer's Table. I carefully placed the pocket watch and the rope inside a cloth bag and looped it over my shoulder.

My father feverishly worked on his painting. The black outline of trees, a lake, and a boardwalk took shape. He dabbed his brush in some green and yellow with a few drops of black and colored in the shingles on the cottage.

I pulled a chair closer to the Writer's Table and opened my notebook. My hands flipped through some of the stories I had written. I examined the letters. The stroke of each character represented more than just ink on paper. It represented incredible kingdoms filled with spectacular people and creatures.

I thought to myself, *Every letter I pen is the ground I walk on, every word I compose is the strength of many, every sentence I devise is the voice of the unspoken, and the stories I write are my worlds of truth.*

When the painting had enough details, I said to my dad, "Okay, now I want you to close your eyes and imagine the cottage and everything in the painting."

He placed the paintbrush down, and as he closed his eyes, I gently pushed him against the table. The familiar burst of light filled the loft, and when it subsided, we were there.

We followed a boardwalk through a tunnel of overgrown hedges. I motioned for my father to follow me. In front of us a double-planked bridge led straight to an old wooden cottage. The cottage sat on a tiny island surrounded by water and dense forest. The house was small but still looked as if it barely fit on the island.

It had a triangular roof, a square bottom, and two windows on either side of the door. On one side was a small evergreen tree that fit perfectly with the setting. The air was cool, and mist clouded beyond the weeping willows that greeted us. Their branches tipped in our direction as if to say hello. This place felt like home.

"Not bad for your first try. What do you think?" I asked.

My father looked all about in awe that he was in the painting he had just created. We made our way up to the cottage door. The water in the pond was clear and still as glass as it reflected the sunless afternoon sky. Clouds and mist rolled overhead.

Inside the cottage was a cozy living room with a quaint little stone fireplace, the kind that sits on the ground and allows you to get as close to it as possible. There was also a tiny loft in the back of the house with two four-post twin-size beds, thick blankets, and deep plush pillows.

"How was all of *this* created? None of these things on the inside of the cottage were in the painting," my father said.

"As you were drawing the outside, I was writing the details on the inside," I said.

"Alden, this is amazing!"

I sat on one of the beds and placed my bag in my lap. I took out the pocket watch and turned it over to read the inscription:

Time is mastered in a series of four
with each taking dichotomy explored.
If you are wise the Guards will see
collecting them all will set us free.

I still didn't know what the inscription meant. Who wrote it? Gather all of what? I suspected it could mean the twelve objects, but I didn't understand how it related to the first part of the inscription. I thought of Tula and wished she were here to help explain.

I ran my thumb over the letters. They were rough and warm to the touch. Just as my finger left the last letter, there was a loud noise coming from outside.

My father and I looked out the window and saw the Writer's Table light up.

With the pocket watch in my hand, we ran downstairs and out to the table, which had a circular rotating light in front of it, like a portal.

I was surprised to see Tula walk through the circle of light. As soon as she saw me, she ran toward me and gave me a big hug.

"Alden!"

"Hey, Tula."

Tula turned and looked at my dad. "You must be Alden's dad. Alden, you did it then! You saved him!"

My father looked confused. "Hi, I'm Jay. Saved me from what, son?"

"Your son found the broken pieces of the pendulum and put everything back in order. Didn't he tell you?"

"I…haven't really had time to tell my dad everything, but don't worry, Dad, we have plenty of time for that," I said. Then I turned to Tula. "I was just looking at the inscription on the back of my pocket watch."

I showed Tula the pocket watch again.

"Tula, when I was with the Macabre, he kept saying Grandpa should have written me better and he eluded that me, Grandpa, and the little girl from the Guardians of Twelve are somehow connected.

Well, he didn't actually confirm that the girl he spoke about was the same girl from the Guardians of Twelve, but then again, he didn't deny it either."

Tula rubbed her thumb in the palm of her hand and looked fidgety.

"What do you think he meant?" I asked Tula.

She looked down at her palm and then stopped rubbing.

"I might know what he meant—although I'm not one hundred percent sure."

"Well, go on and tell me already," I said with eager anticipation.

Tula looked me in the eyes and for a short moment her inquisitive stare examined me, searched my face for a sign that would confirm her suspicions. She then gave my father the same look.

"The twelve objects, as you know, can bring something from the fictional world into your world."

I once again recalled the legendary story from Tula's house and nodded in agreement.

"Well, I think your grandfather somehow obtained all twelve objects and brought something back into your world."

I recalled what the Macabre said.

"The Macabre told me that Grandpa visited the twelve objects."

Tula started rubbing her thumb into her palm again and looked away from me.

"What is it, Tula?" I asked.

"Your grandfather once wrote a story about two children, a boy and a girl, twins. I remembered seeing it many years ago but didn't think anything of it. The story was short and took place in a field surrounded by apple trees. There was an old wooden swing attached to one of the trees, and your grandfather took turns pushing the two children, who squeezed together on the swing."

In my head, I immediately thought, *Not my field with the trees and swing?* It would have been too much of a coincidence that Grandpa and I wrote about the same story.

Tula continued, "The timeline of the story was only for this one day, so again I didn't think much about it. Your grandfather came to me the following morning and said very adamantly that he wanted to scrap the story."

In my quest, I had learned that stories would disappear if the writer stopped visiting or no longer told the story of those people, but never had I stopped to think about what a writer would do if he deliberately wanted to erase a story.

"I agreed to help your grandfather discard the story, sending it to the Wastelands, although I didn't understand why he wanted to get rid of such a beautiful story," Tula said.

There was that reference again. *The Wastelands.* The Macabre said that was where Grandpa was and with the little girl.

"What caught me off guard was that your grandfather said he only wanted a piece of the story to be sent to the Wastelands."

I knew then what Tula would say next, and I felt incredibly shameful.

"He asked that only the little girl be sent to the Wastelands," Tula finished.

I felt terrible that Grandpa would do such a thing. Why would he discard the little girl and not the boy? It didn't seem like the kind of thing he would do.

"So the little girl in the story of the Guardians of Twelve was the little girl from Grandpa's story? How is that possible? Wasn't the story of the Guardians of Twelve prior to Grandpa's existence?" I asked.

"I too thought the same thing. All that I know to be true about our worlds is that the story of the Guardians of Twelve with the little girl and the Macabre was prior to your grandfather's existence, but I also thought the Macabre was destroyed by the little girl, yet he was as alive as you and me in the graveyard. I also thought all of the objects were kept safe, yet your grandfather was able to obtain them."

"What do you think Colvin brought back to our world?" my father asked.

There was a brief moment of silence as Tula and I looked each other in the eyes, and then, as if we had both reached for the last piece of the puzzle, the answered formed.

"The little boy from the story," Tula said. "I think you are that little boy, Alden."

My stomach churned in disbelief. I held my hands out in front of me and dropped the pocket watch on the ground. I turned my hands over, expecting to see right through them. I expected my body to be a hologram.

"After the pendulum was restored, I went back and looked at your grandfather's timeline for the story of the twins and discovered something strange."

I was still in shock that Tula believed I was the fictional boy from Grandpa's story. How could anything else share that level of strangeness?

"There were two other people in that story. A man and a woman. After the little girl was sent to the Wastelands, the man and woman, along with the little boy, disappeared from the story as well, but they were not sent to the Wastelands, which I confirmed in the register. They seemed to have disappeared completely."

If Tula thought I was that little boy and Grandpa brought me back to the real world, then that meant—

"I think the man is you, Jay, and the woman is your wife."

What Tula was saying couldn't be true. Not only did she think I was fictional but my parents too.

"Can you tell me anything about your childhood prior to the age of eight?" Tula asked.

"Of course I can remember my life before I was eight. I was born in Dunes City, Oregon, I'm eight years old, and my favorite childhood memory is our trip to the Redwood Forest."

"What else can you tell me?"

I searched my mind and could only recall three memories.

"I remembered my first encounter with the Writer's Table, when it cut my hand; an evening in the summer when Grandpa made me ice cream and read me *The Lonely Tree*; and—"

"The story of Dexas?" Tula interrupted.

"Yes—how did you know?"

"It was all part of your story. It's all in his register," she said.

I tried to think as far back as possible, but nothing came to mind.

"Perhaps you can't remember because your grandfather didn't write any memories for you before the age of eight."

"He was always asking me the same three questions every time I saw him."

"He was probably making sure you were still the character he wrote. The writer can make their characters have select memories, the memories they choose to write."

I put my hands over my face. The disbelief and the questions flooded my head. Did I own any part of me? Was everything about me fake?

Tula picked up the pocket watch.

"And Alden—I think this inscription was meant for you, a message from your grandfather."

I slowly dropped my hands to my side and looked back at Tula. She recited the inscription out loud:

Time is mastered in a series of four
with each taking dichotomy explored.
If you are wise the Guards will see
collecting them all will set us free.

"But what does it mean?" I asked.

"'Time is mastered in a series of four.'. If you look at the face of a clock, twelve through three is a quarter of time—a series of four.

"'With each taking dichotomy explored.' I'm not sure about this one. Maybe something good and something bad will happen?

"'If you are wise the Guards will see collecting them all will set us free.' I think this is referring to the twelve objects and perhaps we can free your Grandpa from the Wastelands once we have all of them."

My head wanted to explode with all of the new information. I felt the same way I did when Babacan told me everything about the time change and Grandpa's adventures. It was a lot to take in one sitting. I just finished finding the pieces of the pendulum and now Tula wanted me to somehow take the twelve objects and use them to free Grandpa from the Wastelands.

"You need to get to your grandfather and get your questions answered. Don't you want to know why he chose you and not the little girl? Don't you want to know why he chose your mom and dad?"

"How will we get the twelve objects?" I asked.

She glanced over her shoulder at the Writer's Table. At that very moment, one of the drawers in the hutch opened and the knob attached twisted in place. The knob popped out onto the ground. It was attached to something long with bristles at one end.

"What is it?" my father asked.

I walked over and picked it up. "It's a paint brush."

ACKNOWLEDGMENTS

I want to thank my wonderful team of editors, Abby Abell, Dylan Sharek, and Jennifer Zaczek, for the substantial feedback and support you gave me on the book.

Thank you to my friend and cover designer, Megan Katsanevakis. I'm amazed at how fate brought us together on this project—you are an amazing designer and visionary!

I'm also so grateful for the design team, Julie Atwood, Brianne Twilley, Danna Mathias, and Becca Curtis, for giving me the opportunity to see such incredible design options.

Thank you to my large family for entertaining my kids while I spent many nights writing late.

To my amazing Artisery group, Morgan East and Laura Polson, for keeping the dream alive. Thank you again, Morgan, for creating the vision I had for the image of the writing table—your Photoshop skills are far beyond mine. Laura thanks for the professional photos for my social media accounts. You made me look less weird.

Thank you to my beta readers, Nadeen Bir, Amber Nungesser, Colleen Serreno, Olivia Summerfield, Vashti Summerfield, Caryn Perkins, and Roy Wyzykiewicz. Your dedication and feedback pushed me even further with the story.

Finally, to all the storytellers out there: find your own Writer's Table and bring your stories to life. Don't let them go undiscovered!

ABOUT THE AUTHOR

Julian Simmons is an accomplished traveler to imaginative worlds. He is also a recording artist and has performed at New York's prestigious Carnegie Hall. Simmons enjoys reading for local schools and teaching kids how to write stories of their own. For more information about the author and *The Writer's Table* please visit www.juliansimmonsbooks.com

Made in the USA
Charleston, SC
09 May 2016